Death and the Trumpets of Tuscany

By Hazel Wynn Jones
DEATH AND THE TRUMPETS OF TUSCANY
THE FLYING SORCERER

Death and the Trumpets of Tuscany

HAZEL WYNN JONES

A Crime Club Book
Doubleday
NEW YORK   LONDON   TORONTO   SYDNEY   AUCKLAND

A Crime Club Book
Published by Doubleday, a division of
Bantam Doubleday Dell Publishing Group, Inc.
666 Fifth Avenue, New York, New York 10103

Doubleday and the portrayal of a man
with a gun are trademarks of
Doubleday, a division of Bantam Doubleday Dell
Publishing Group, Inc.

Library of Congress Cataloging-in-Publication Data

Jones, Hazel Wynn.
Death and the trumpets of Tuscany/Hazel Wynn Jones.
p.   cm.
"A Crime Club book."
I. Title.
PR6060.05164D4   1989
823'.914—dc19   89-31314
CIP

ISBN 0-385-26198-5
Copyright © 1988 by Hazel Wynn Jones
All Rights Reserved
Printed in the United States of America
October 1989

THE TRUMPETS OF TUSCANY

Leading Players

STELLA CAMAY
RICHARD TRAHERNE
BROCK BEROWNE
LEONIDAS
ARIADNE

YORKY, stunt double for Richard
DAVE and JOHNNY, leading stunt men

Film Unit

HAL, First Assistant Director
MARCO, Second Assistant Director
EMMA, Continuity Girl
LUCIANO, Art Director
FRANTIŠEK, Lighting Cameraman
BETH, Wardrobe
BABS, Hairdresser
CHARLES, Makeup
FRANK JONES, Production Manager
PENNY, Production Secretary

Script by L. J. HACKER
Associate Producer WALTHER MEISTER
Produced and Directed by KARL MEISTER

PLUS
Commissario GABRIELI of the Venice Questura
CALVI, his assistant

AND
STEPHEN LOVELACE, an outsider

Death and the Trumpets of Tuscany

1

"Silenzio! Si gira! ACTION!"

The fifties were good times for film-makers in Italy. Rome was Hollywood-on-the-Tiber. The gates of Cinecittà were perpetually besieged by hordes of would-be extras who had been employed on *Quo Vadis* and who refused to believe that their services were no longer required. ("But, signorina, I was crucified next to St. Peter!") At times it seemed as though the whole of Italy was one vast film studio. At this very moment William Wyler was filming on the streets of Rome with Audrey Hepburn and Gregory Peck, John Huston was filming at Ravello with Gina Lollobrigida and Humphrey Bogart, and here in Venice, Karl Meister was about to begin shooting on *The Trumpets of Tuscany*, starring Richard Traherne, Stella Camay, and a guest star, uninvited and unwelcome, whose name was Death.

It was a pleasant evening in the Piazza San Marco. The English members of Karl Meister's crew had re-named the film *The Strumpets of Tuscany*, and were hopefully eyeing the local talent, which was returning the compliment, but more discreetly. Among the professionals making their first early evening circuit were several young ladies from the house called "Clara's." One of their number had recently left to marry a man who was going to get her into pictures, so they took a very particular interest in the film people who were scattered about the Piazza, and who were not hard to identify. There was a large contingent from Rome consisting of electricians, carpenters, painters and plasterers: good-humoured and noisy, emphasizing their conversation with dramatic gestures. There were two Americans with biscuit-coloured complexions and matching lightweight biscuit-coloured suits. And there were the English, looking uncomfortably red from too much unaccustomed sunshine, and justifying their common Italian nickname of *"Bistecca,"* meaning beefsteak. One of these was Hal Halliwell, a large, fair-haired man in his early thirties, so big and broad that the Italian members of the crew had already nicknamed him *"Il Bisteccone,"* the *Big* Beefsteak. Hal sat alone and stared gloomily at the crushed ice in the tall glass in front of him.

He didn't give a second glance to the soaring Campanile, or the Basilica with its domes and great bronze horses. He had seen it all when he first arrived a few weeks ago, and now he accepted the Piazza as though it were a film set. High above him, the two blackamoors of the Orologio stood silhouetted against the pale green of the evening sky, their hammers raised to strike the bronze bell. The sun was still warm, but already there were soft lights gleaming in the shop-windows. Hal saw a familiar figure walking across the Piazza. Emma Shaw, Continuity Girl. Elegant Italian clothes. Dark hair tumbling over her forehead in feathery curls. Small, lively and bright-eyed, a girl he could have fallen for if she hadn't been so regrettably dedicated to her work. He couldn't remember ever hearing Emma talk about anything but film-making. Still, she could provide him with the information he wanted. He waved, and she came hurrying towards him.

"Ciao, Hal!"

He pulled out a chair for her.

"This is my first chance of talking to you," he said.

"It's been hectic these last few weeks," said Emma. "Karl's an absolute slave-driver—and he's only *preparing* the picture. I hate to think what he'll be like when we begin shooting."

"The same, but more so," said Hal. "I worked for him once, four years ago. He was a bastard then, and he's a bastard now."

"When Karl interviewed me for this job," said Emma, "he

talked about film-making so beautifully that I felt like crying. I could have lain down on the floor and let him walk all over me."

"And now?" said Hal.

"Now," said Emma ruefully, "I realize that Karl has every intention of doing just that—and not just walking over me, but stamping about in great big hobnailed boots."

"He does it to everyone," said Hal. "Still, he's a damned good director. Not like that idiot in the film we worked on together in England—how long ago was that?"

"Two years," said Emma, a little too quickly.

It was on that film that she had first met Hal, and had fallen in love with him. But Hal was married, and Emma was a nice, if inexperienced, young woman, so she had put on a show of indifference, adopted a brisk professional manner, and whenever she spoke to Hal was careful to talk of nothing but film-making.

"What have you been doing since then?" asked Hal.

"I came out to Italy on a film being made in Assisi," said Emma. "When that finished, they asked me to stay on for another picture, and then another. I've got an apartment in Rome now. The Americans are making so many pictures here, there always seems to be plenty of work going."

(Enough to fool me into thinking I'd forgotten you, my dear. And now you've come back into my life, and the pain is going to start all over again. What could be more romantic than Venice with Hal? And what was going to be utterly *unro-mantic*? Venice with Hal, plus Karl Meister.)

He glanced down at her left hand. No wedding ring.

"You're not married?" he said.

"No," she said. "And you?"

"Married. Cuckolded. Divorced." Hal spoke harshly.

"Oh, I—I'm sorry—I didn't know . . ." Her heart missed a beat.

"No reason why you should. It's all over now. Hard to stay

married in this business. Always working odd hours, or going off on location for months on end. Coming back unexpectedly to find a cuckoo in the nest . . ."

They were both silent for a few minutes. A waiter arrived, and Hal ordered a Cinzano for Emma.

"When did you learn Italian?" he said.

"I had some lessons in England, but most of it I picked up over here," said Emma. "Marco was very useful—he was on the Assisi film, and he wanted to learn English technical terms in film-making, so we helped each other."

"Tell me about Marco," said Hal. This was the information he wanted. "Will he be a help or a hindrance? He's supposed to be my assistant, but he looks much too young."

"He's about twenty, and he's a good worker," said Emma.

"Reliable?" said Hal. "Not likely to go to pieces in a crisis? The last time I worked with Karl Meister he gave my assistant a nervous breakdown."

"No, Marco's all right," said Emma. "I gather he comes from a very old family which lost everything in the war. His parents died when he was quite young, and he had to fend for himself. He's tougher than he looks. There he is now, over by the Campanile."

Hal turned, and saw Marco walking towards them. A slight young man, wearing his casual clothes with an air of elegance. An olive skin, an oval face, a carefree smile. A pleasant young man. But would he have the stamina to cope with a director like Karl Meister? Hal looked across the crowded Piazza to a table outside the most expensive café in Venice, where Karl Meister, producer and director of *The Trumpets of Tuscany*, was the centre of attention.

Karl's was a hobgoblin's face, with black eyes snapping under fierce black eyebrows. A heavy gold wedding ring. A slim gold watch. A well-to-do hobgoblin. And at the moment, an unhappy one. He was cursing himself for making this stupid picture when he might have been at home in Santa Monica with his wife. Minna always came with him when he was filming, and provided a soothing background for him to crawl into at the end of the day's work. But Minna was in San Francisco, where their only daughter was about to have her first baby. Karl glared at the crowds in the Piazza, and hated them all.

Then he rested his hand on the shoulder of his cousin Walther, and felt a little better. Karl looked up to Walther as he had done ever since he was a very small boy and Walther his big cousin. Indeed, Karl's devotion to Walther was one of the few endearing things about him, and it was one that most people who worked with him would have swopped for something else even more endearing, like stopping work at the proper time for a lunch-break, or paying his round instead of sliding off and leaving somebody else to pick up the tab. Walther was a larger, handsomer version of Karl. No wedding ring for Walther. A few brown age-spots on his hands, but his face smooth and unlined, the face of a man accustomed to an easy life. Over the past sixty years Walther had consistently said and done foolish things that only a mother could forgive, but the great Karl Meister was devoted to him, so Walther was a man who could get away with murder.

The third man at the table was L. J. Hacker. Back home in London he was highly regarded as a writer of English domestic comedies, but last year a film he had scripted had had an unexpected success in the States. There had even been talk (which came to nothing) that the script might be nominated for an Oscar, and on the strength of that talk Walther Meister, Associate Producer, with one of his flashes of inspiration that so often turned out to be misguided, had signed up L. J. Hacker to write the final script of *The Trumpets of Tuscany*, a colourful, action-packed story of mediaeval Italy. Hacker had been wildly excited at the prospect, particularly when it was made clear that he would have to accompany the film unit on location, and that the management would pay his expenses. So he and his wife had arrived in Venice, where Mr. Hacker put the finishing touches to his script and Mrs. Hacker complained about the heat, the mosquitoes, the smell from the canals and the high cost of sending postcards to England. L. J. Hacker had presented his finished script to Walther, who had passed it to Karl, who had invited him to discuss the script over a drink in the Piazza San Marco. Karl had given his opinion on a number of subjects, and Walther had agreed with him, but so far neither of them had mentioned *The Trumpets of Tuscany*.

"I must have been mad to come here," said Hacker to himself, for the twentieth time in as many days. Aloud he said, "If you'll excuse me, Karl, I'd better get back to the hotel and see how Winifred is—she had rather a nasty headache when I came out."

"You do that, Hack," said Karl, and smiled with all the charm of a barracuda. The gibe went home, and Hacker froze. "Hack" indeed, to a script-writer who had almost been nominated for an Oscar!

Karl turned to his cousin and murmured something which made Walther laugh. They rose like a pair of Siamese twins and headed for their hotel. At that moment a waiter arrived and presented the bill to Hacker. Karl Meister was running true to form. He had invited Hacker for a drink at the most expensive place in the Piazza San Marco, and had left him to pick up the tab.

The next morning, Stephen Lovelace arrived at the Palazzo Pavone. The ancient Palazzo had seen better days, but it had also seen worse ones, so Karl Meister had been able to rent the entire building for several weeks at a price that even he considered reasonable. Stephen timidly pushed open the heavy wooden door and stepped from the street into the courtyard, and the organized chaos of an Italian film set. Carpenters hammered and sang at their work, painters painted and whistled, electricians manhandled enormous lamps or trailed thick black cables over the antique brick floor. Groups of men battled to hang up a series of canvas tapestries designed to hide the lighting gantries and at the same time create an atmosphere of mediaeval Venice. Framed in the far doorway, with the sunlit waters of the canal behind him, stood a large fair-haired man, looking superbly self-confident. Stephen felt out of place and was tempted to slink away before anyone noticed him, but he was too late. A young woman was coming towards him, and when she smiled, Stephen decided to stay.

"Ciao!" she said. "You must be Stephen Lovelace. I'm Emma, Karl's Continuity Girl."

She took him up a broad flight of stone stairs and ushered him into Karl Meister's office. As she closed the door, she heard Stephen say, "M-Mr. Meister, your film is called *The T-Trumpets of Tuscany,* so why are you making it in V-Venice?"

Emma winced. She felt sorry for the young man. His skin was pale, his clothes were wrong, he looked like a bewildered baby owl. She gave him five minutes.

Karl gave him four. The door of his office opened abruptly and Stephen came out.

"Emma," said Karl, "Mr. Lovelace is writing a book about the making of the film. Look after him. And take this goddam crap to the Hack."

He thrust some script pages into her hand and went down the stairs. They watched him charge through the crowded courtyard and out on to the landing-stage of the canal.

"Come on," said Emma, and led Stephen up a flight of stairs to the next floor, where there were several rooms with their doors firmly closed.

"Star dressing-rooms," she said, and took him up a narrower flight of stairs to the next floor.

"Art Department," she said.

Stephen saw an open doorway, and in the room beyond it a number of people clustered round a drawing-board. An argument seemed to be in progress.

She led him up to the next floor.

"Hairdressing, Make-Up and Wardrobe," she said.

Through the open doorways Stephen caught glimpses of

bright lights and mirrors, of wigs on stands, costumes hanging on rails, a washing-machine churning, and somebody standing at an ironing-board. There was a general smell of make-up, spirit gum, shampoo and dry-cleaning fluid, and overall a smell of scorching accompanied by sudden shrill cries.

Emma hurried Stephen up another flight of stairs. Two very large rooms were filled with extras in various stages of dress, making enough noise for a small war. Emma paused, then went towards a cupboard in a small, dark corner. She tapped on the door.

"Come!" said the magisterial voice of L. J. Hacker.

Emma put her head round the door—there was no room for the rest of her. The script-writer's office held a chair, a table with a typewriter, and L. J. Hacker, who luckily was a small man.

"Karl asked me to give you these pages, Mr. Hacker," she said.

"Thank you, Emma," said L. J. Hacker.

Emma turned away and led Stephen down the stairs again.

"It sounds rather rude to call M-Mr. Hacker 'Hack,' you know," he said. "Do you think M-Mr. Meister realizes that 'hack' is a w-word for a—w-well, a not very g-good writer?"

"I'm sure he does," said Emma. "That's why he uses it. He's not a nice man. Still, we call *him* 'Karl the Snarl,' though not to his face. We start shooting this evening, and we'll probably have some more names for him before long."

"This isn't a bit how I imagined f-films were m-made," said Stephen sadly.

Emma laughed.

"Oh, we're just one big happy family," she said. "Every now and then we all feel like murdering each other, but we never do it, so don't worry."

They reached the foot of the staircase, and Emma started across the courtyard. Stephen followed. He noticed a minia-ture railway track on which squatted a heavy black camera. The camera suddenly ran forward and nearly mowed him down. Instead of apologizing, the camera crew yelled at him to get out of the way. He got out of the way and tripped over a heap of cables, bumped into a group of men trying to haul a thirty-foot-high curtain up against a wall, got shouted at again, stepped back and found himself in the middle of a sword-fight which had spilled out from below the balustrade, got shouted at again, and at last reached the safety of Emma's desk, marvelling at the ease with which Emma threaded her way through all these obstacles without apparently noticing them.

The tall fair-haired man came in from the canal.

"Lunch-break!" he shouted. "One hour . . ."

"Pausa!" called another voice. *"Un' ora . . ."*

The confusion in the courtyard came to a stop. The camera was pulled back to the start of the track and locked in position; the stunt men retired under the balustrade; the gang hauling up the curtain left it to its own devices, so that it collapsed like a deflated balloon; electricians came swarming down from the gantries, and carpenters and painters appeared from all sides. Everyone was heading for the corner near the street-door where cardboard lunch-boxes were being handed out. People sat wherever they could and began to eat and drink, and soon the whole courtyard looked like a great picnic. Some people sat on the stairs, and the Hairdressing, Make-Up and Wardrobe staff had to squeeze their way past as they came down to collect their lunch. Emma could hear the distant thunder of a horde of extras coming down from their dressing-rooms on the top floor.

"We'd better get our lunch-boxes," she said, "or there'll be none left."

Stephen hung back, suddenly shy. Emma collected two lunch-boxes, and offered him one. He opened it cautiously. He found cold spaghetti, cold chicken, a salad, an apple, a piece of cheese, and a sugar-topped pastry.

"This looks g-great!" he said. "Do you g-get this every day?"

"Afraid so," said Emma. "They do their best to ring the changes, but really it's always the same thing: cold pasta, cold meat and salad, and always, always the pastry with the sugar on top."

Stephen took a bite of the pastry. The loose powdery sugar fell off and landed in a small snowstorm all over his pants. He licked his fingers, dabbed up all the sugar and licked it off. Then he went on to the chicken and salad.

The large fair-haired man came towards them, and Emma's heart gave a little flip, as it always did whenever Hal came near. As always, she repressed it firmly. Theirs would never be more than a professional relationship.

"Oh, Hal," she said, "this is Stephen. He's writing a book about the film."

Karl Meister suddenly appeared in the canal doorway with his cousin Walther. They brought with them a strong and unpleasant smell from the canal.

"Where's my lunch?" roared Karl.

"Who's been eating *my* porridge?" murmured Emma, and Stephen laughed and nearly choked himself. A slender young Italian moved quickly across the courtyard towards Karl and Walther.

"Your lunch is ready for you in your office, Mr. Meister," he said.

"I want lunch out here on the goddam landing-stage," said Karl.

"Yes, Mr. Meister," said the young man politely.

He went back across the courtyard and collected two lunch-boxes only to find when he turned round that Karl and Walther were charging up the great staircase, scattering the seated picnickers as they went.

"Leave it, Marco!" shouted Karl. "We'll eat in the office."

He went on up the stairs. Walther followed him, and they entered their respective offices. The picnickers settled down again. Marco laughed as he walked over to Emma's desk with the two lunch-boxes. He gave one to Hal, and they settled down to have lunch.

"Stephen," said Emma, "this is Marco, Second Assistant Director. Marco, this is Stephen. He's going to write a book about the making of the film."

"*Ciao,* Stephen!" said Marco. "I would like to be a writer, but I would not like to write books, I would like to write film scripts."

"What Marco really wants," said Emma, "is to be a film producer."

"Of course," said Marco. "I would like to write the script and then produce the film so that it is made the way I want it, not the way some stupid film director wants to make it. Emma, of course, wants to be a stupid film director."

"Not a stupid one, Marco," said Emma. "I want to be a *good* film director."

They smiled at each other. It was not the first time they had had this conversation.

"I'm never quite sure," said Stephen, "what's the d-difference between a p-producer and a d-director?"

"The producer is the most important person," said Marco hastily. "He decides which story shall be made into a film, what money shall be spent on it, who shall direct it and who the stars will be. He is the man who has the last word—he is the man who has the power."

"The director is the most important person," said Emma, "because he—or she—actually creates the picture."

Hal said, "The producer is like the boss of a shipping line. He owns the ships—he decides where to send them—what cargoes they are to carry. The director is like the captain of one of the ships. He makes all the decisions during the voyage. But once the voyage is over, he's out of a job. Marco wants to be like the ship-owner, Emma wants to be like the captain. But you haven't a hope in hell, Emma, you know that."

"Why not?" flared Emma. "I've worked with some of the

best directors in the business. I've seen how they get results. I know how a film is organized. I know how it's edited. And what's more I *know* I can do it!"

They glared at each other. It was not the first time they had had *this* conversation either.

"Emma, you know as well as I do, no producer would give a woman a job as a director," said Hal flatly.

"I would," said Marco, and the angry tension between Emma and Hal evaporated.

"Have you written many books, Stephen?" asked Marco.

"This is my f-first," said Stephen. "You see, I met M-Mr. Meister in London some time ago when he was g-giving a lecture—I'm terribly k-keen on his films—and afterwards—I d-don't quite know how it happened, b-but I said I'd love to see how he m-made a film—and then write a b-book about it. And M-Mr. Meister said why didn't I d-do just that. He said he'd start filming in V-Venice this week, so last week I left my job, drew out my savings, and h-here I am."

The others stared at him as if he were a rare specimen.

"Have you got a publisher for your book?" asked Emma.

"Well, n-no," said Stephen. "I thought I'd b-better write it first, and then find a p-publisher."

"What are you going to live on while you're writing it?" asked Hal.

Stephen was silent.

"Do you mean to say," said Emma, "that you've thrown up your job, blued your savings, and come out here simply on the word of Karl Meister?"

"Well, y-yes," said Stephen. "I suppose I h-have."

"Did you ask Mr. Meister to pay your expenses while you're out here?" she asked.

"Oh, no," said Stephen. "I didn't want to take advantage of M-Mr. Meister."

"You didn't want to take advantage of Mr. Meister," said Hal. He sighed. "That'll be the frosty Friday."

2

Karl spent the afternoon rehearsing the opening scene on the canal. As soon as it was dark he began shooting. Emma, standing beside the camera on a balcony overhanging the canal, thought the scene looked very impressive. Torches flared from the high stone walls and were reflected in the smooth waters of the canal. Light spilled from the windows of the Palazzo Pavone, and torches blazed above the landing-stage. More light poured out through the doorway that led to the courtyard. Extras dressed as revellers in fantastic costumes and masks were penned up in the courtyard, waiting to revel when required. At the moment they were only required to sit around and keep reasonably quiet. They were managing to sit around quite creditably, but they were not keeping quiet. Stephen crept up on to the balcony with his notebook and pencil and tried to keep out of everyone's way while seeing what was going on. Naturally, he got in everyone's way and didn't see much of what was going on.

Hal and Marco were below in two small boats, doing their best to control the thirty gondolas waiting to make their grand entrance. Each gondola contained one or two extras wearing fantastic costumes. Some sat bolt upright and gripped the sides of the boat, terrified of falling into the water. Others lay back on the cushions with their partners and made the most of their opportunities.

"Is that Stella Camay down there in the g-gondola?" asked Stephen.

"No, it's her stand-in," said Emma. "We're too far away to see her in this shot. And anyway the stand-in will have her mask up to her face—you could have Boris Karloff behind that mask and nobody would ever know."

Shooting began. The first gondola came gliding into the picture from below the camera, followed by a string of boats, each with a lantern swinging and scattering patches of light over the dark water. The first gondola swung right towards the Palazzo landing-stage, where the revellers were milling about under flaring torches and moving through the lighted doorway into the courtyard beyond. The first gondolier moored his boat to the landing-stage, his passenger leaped nimbly ashore, slipped on the seaweed and fell into the canal.

"Cut!" shouted Karl. "Get 'em back again, Hal. Move it! We haven't got all night . . ."

Marco fished out the unfortunate extra and sent him off to Wardrobe. Another extra replaced the wet one, and the fleet of gondolas gathered itself together and moved back to its position under the balcony.

It took about three hours to get the shot. The camera had to be re-loaded. The torches had to be re-lit. A party of German tourists in a vaporetto entered the canal by mistake and decided to stay and watch the filming, until Karl screamed at them in his native tongue. And on the first occasion that all the boats and all the extras performed perfectly, Walther appeared on the landing-stage, waved up at the balcony and called out, "You can't see me here, can you?" They could. Stephen expected another outburst at this, but Karl merely laughed indulgently.

At last the scene was finished, and Hal sent Marco to call Stella Camay. Marco moved easily through the throng of chattering extras and up two flights of stairs to the star dressing-room.

"Ready for you now, Miss Camay," he called.

"Come in, Marco," called Stella.

He went in. Stella was small and blonde, with the delicate cameo profile which had inspired her first agent, many years ago, to change her name from something unpronounceable to something as easy on the eye as Stella herself. "Mitsouko" perfume hung in the air, drifting as she moved towards him. She looked unbelievably fragile, and Marco caught his breath audibly and stooped to kiss her hand. Stella looked down at his bowed head. She liked her men handsome, husky and rough, and Marco was none of these things, but he was an attractive young man. She smiled and rested one hand lightly on his arm, while with the other she gathered up the long skirt of her gown. Marco picked up her gilded mask and escorted her from the room.

Seated at her desk in the courtyard, Emma looked up and saw Marco and Stella coming down the great staircase. They made a handsome pair—Stella like a confection of spun-glass, and Marco moving with an aristocratic air at odds with his working clothes. They descended the staircase in a stately fashion, the extras falling back to give them room. At the foot of the stairs Marco smiled gravely, handed Stella her mask, and then melted away. Beth Wardrobe, Babs Hairdresser and Charles Make-Up gathered round Stella for last-minute tweaking, powdering and checking in the mirror. Emma grabbed her script and hurried to join Karl and the camera crew on the landing-stage. Stella arrived with her entourage, and Stephen hovered in the background.

"Stella," said Karl, "you're in the gondola on your way to the revels. We're shooting without sound, so I'll talk you through. Where's the goddam gondolier?"

"He's here, Karl," said Emma.

The gondolier was handsome, husky and rough. He wore his mediaeval costume with a swagger, and Emma noticed that the swagger became more pronounced when he caught sight of Stella Camay. She looked him over slowly. Their eyes met, and held.

Then the gondolier stepped into his boat and helped Stella in. A second boat, containing the camera and the camera crew, had been lashed to Stella's gondola. Karl and Emma stepped into it, and the double craft moved out to the middle of the canal. At a signal from Karl the boats slowed down until they were almost stationary. Hal and Marco remained on the landing-stage, watching.

Shooting began.

"Take away the mask now, Stella," said Karl. "Now—a little smile—you're looking forward to the revels—now put the mask on again—now just peep round it—put the mask down— you wonder—are you really going to enjoy the revels after all?"

Stella did as she was told.

"Cut," said Karl. "Print it."

He turned to the operator.

"Big close-up now, Bob."

Bob gave a slight nod, and his assistant slipped a softening filter in front of the camera lens.

Stella lay back on her silken cushions and looked up at the gondolier. She opened her blue eyes very wide, and the blue suddenly seemed to intensify. Emma smiled to see the gondolier react as though the effect was intended for him alone. It was a professional trick of Stella's, preparing for her big close-up, and it was intended for audiences all over the world.

"Shooting now, Stella," said Karl softly. "You're in big close-up. Raise your mask and cover your face—slowly—now take the mask away and think about—Love . . ."

"Wow!" said the camera operator to himself, as he got the full force of Stella's intensely blue eyes thinking about Love. He gave Karl the thumbs-up sign.

"Cut and print," said Karl. "Back to the landing-stage. Come on, come on, move it, we haven't got all night . . ."

"Dinner-break! One hour!" called Hal.

"Pausa! Un' ora!" called Marco.

The courtyard was once more a general picnic area. Emma gulped her coffee and began typing up her notes of the evening's shooting. Marco put his head round the canal doorway and shouted for quiet.

"Silenzio, per favore!"

Emma stopped typing. The chatter of the picnickers subsided slightly, and Marco disappeared.

Stella came sweeping down the stairs.

"What's happening, Emma?" she asked.

"They're shooting a wild track of the gondolas on the canal," said Emma.

"Can I peep?" said Stella.

She didn't wait for an answer, but walked towards the canal doorway. Stephen hurried over and opened the heavy door for her. She stepped outside, and Stephen followed.

Marco was standing on the landing-stage with the sound crew. He turned angrily, and gestured to Stephen to shut the door. The microphone was suspended by a kind of fishing-rod over the gently lapping water of the canal. At a signal from Marco the first gondola moved forward through the darkness, cutting through the water, the oar creaking. There was a gentle bumping sound as the gondola paused at the landing-stage, then there was the sound of the oar creaking and the boat moving away. The other gondolas followed, like a fleet of black swans, the silence broken only by the creak of oars and the sound of the boats moving through the water. The last boat disappeared into the darkness. Gerry the Sound Recordist removed his headphones and nodded to Marco, who called the boats back and dismissed them.

"Which is my gondola, Marco?" asked Stella, resting one hand lightly on his shoulder and peering at the mass of boats moving away.

"That one," said Marco, "the one with the blue cushions."

He turned away to speak to the sound crew, so Stephen was the only person to notice that Stella gave a charming little wave of her hand in the direction of the boat with the blue cushions, and that the husky gondolier responded with a rather more vigorous signal.

Within a few days the unit had settled into its routine, and Stephen had settled with it. Part of the routine was that he and Hal and Marco should gather round Emma's desk for their lunch-break. One day they had worked their way through their lunch-boxes, and now only Stephen had anything left to eat. It was his favourite, the sugar-topped pastry.

Stella Camay came down the stairs and moved towards them.

"Hal, you don't want me this afternoon, do you?" she asked. But it was Marco she was looking at.

"No," said Hal. "We shan't get to your scenes today. Your call is 8:30 tomorrow morning."

"Thanks, doll," said Stella absently. "I'll have myself a little fun this afternoon." She looked at Marco and smiled. "While you're working, you can think of me enjoying myself."

She looked down at the four lunch-boxes, empty except for Stephen's pastry. She leaned forward, picked up the pastry and ate it, taking tiny little bites and all the time looking at Marco through half-closed eyes. They all watched in silence as she scattered the usual snowstorm of powdered sugar over Emma's desk, and then wetted her fingers and chased the white specks until she had gathered them all up. Then with dainty flicks of her tongue she licked her fingers clean, like a pretty little cat.

"Thank you, Marco," she said. "Oh, would you see if my gondola has arrived?"

Marco put down his cup and went out to the landing-stage, then returned and escorted Stella to the boat with the blue cushions. The husky gondolier moved off at once as though he had no need to ask their destination.

Hal and Emma looked at each other.

"Well!" said Emma. "If that means what I think it means—"

"Damn Stella!" said Hal. "Marco's too good to be baited like that by a greedy woman—"

"It wasn't Marco's pastry, it was mine," said Stephen angrily. "I was saving it till last." Clearly the significance of the scene had escaped him. "Oh, Hal, I meant to ask you—who's playing opposite Stella?"

"Richard Traherne," said Hal.

"Richard Tra—!" said Stephen. "B-but he was p-playing leads in the thirties! I m-mean—he must be—over forty years old!"

"Thirty-five, according to my calculations," said the voice of Richard Traherne close behind him.

Stephen turned scarlet and felt about an inch high.

Richard Traherne smiled gently, showing beautiful white teeth. Even without make-up he was a handsome man, with deep blue eyes under devil-may-care eyebrows. Impressionable young women wove romantic dreams about him, just as their mothers and aunts had done some twenty years earlier. He was carrying a single red rose in a cardboard cup which he placed on Emma's already overcrowded desk.

"Lovely!" said Emma. "Thank you, Richard."

"If only the script would smell as sweet," said Richard, and walked away. They watched him moving lightly up the great staircase.

"He's a nice man to work with," said Emma. "A complete Hollywood professional. Gets to work on time, knows his lines, keeps himself fit."

"And never has any entanglements," said Hal, clearly still angry with Stella. "He told me the other day that he still has the same wife, the same agent and the same accountant that he started with. And the same stunt double—Yorky."

"Perhaps that's why he can still play young—well, youngish —heroes," said Emma. "Wherever he goes, his people are always the same. They're like a cocoon around him."

For a moment she wondered what would happen if that orderly pattern of existence were threatened and the insulating cocoon broken. What would happen when, even by Richard's calculations, his age was no longer thirty-five?

"Who's playing the villain?" asked Stephen.

"Oh, that's Brock Berowne," said Emma.

"B-Brock Berowne—he's the English actor with the white streak in his h-hair, isn't he?" said Stephen.

"That's right," said Emma. "Black hair, white streak like a badger—hence the name Brock, I suppose. He's not on call for quite a while. Won't be here for at least another week."

But there she was wrong.

That evening she was walking across the Piazza San Marco, taking time to enjoy the music and the lights, when she saw a figure that was vaguely familiar. A handsome man with a streak of white in his dark hair. Brock Berowne.

"Emma!"

Brock recognized her with a joyful shout, and waved like a drowning man. Never had an actor been so glad to see a Continuity Girl approaching. She hurried over to his table.

"Good God, Brock, what are you doing here? You aren't on call for ages!"

"Emma, I'm broke, I'm lost, I'm desperate, I'm starving!"

She sat down opposite him. A waiter appeared. She ordered a cognac for herself, and coffee and some food for Brock. When the waiter returned, Brock drank the cognac and Emma found herself drinking the coffee.

"But why are you *here*, Brock?" she asked.

"My agent got a call from the Rome office to send me over immediately for a wardrobe fitting. I caught a plane to Rome at some ungodly hour, had my costume fittings, and then they put me on a train to Venice and said somebody would meet me and fix me up with a hotel and money."

"And nobody met you."

"Right."

"Why didn't you go straight to the Production Office?"

"I don't know where it is."

Emma stared at him. Actors would never cease to astonish her. Brock Berowne had had a roaring success in the West End as Richard III, and at Stratford upon Avon he had been a dashing Petruchio, a towering Shylock and a monumental Othello. Yet Brock Berowne, at a phone call from his agent, or more likely from his agent's secretary, had meekly travelled to Rome and then to Venice with nothing but the clothes he stood up in, and no idea of where he was going.

"I was beginning to think," said Brock, "that I'd have to sell myself for the price of a bed and breakfast." He grinned. "There's a lady at that table over there who was beginning to look as though she might be interested . . ."

Emma noticed that a hint of Petruchio had appeared. She couldn't blame the lady for looking interested. Brock was a very attractive man. All the same, she was completely taken by surprise when Brock leaned across the table, took both her hands in his, and said softly, "You, my dear Emma, can have me for free . . . if you'll have me?"

He looked at her, and her blood started to pound. She could see nothing but Brock's face, his dark eyes holding hers.

It would be so easy to give in. Close your eyes, Emma, and think it's Hal . . . She caught a sudden flash of triumph in Brock's eyes, and recognized the look. He was Richard III wooing Queen Anne. "Was ever woman in this humour woo'd?" Was ever woman in this humour won?"

"Not this woman," she said to herself, and came firmly back to earth. She shook her head regretfully.

"I'm sorry, Brock," she said.

"Someone else?" said Brock.

She nodded. What could she say? "I'm in love with Hal, and he regards me as a dedicated member of the crew, nothing more."

She stood up.

"Come on, Brock, let's get moving before the Production Office closes."

She paid the bill and hauled him to his feet, leading him across the darkening Piazza. Suddenly Brock halted.

"Emma," he said, "I have just made a very important discovery. Until now, this has all been somewhere at the end of an extremely tedious railway journey. But it is beautiful—it is glorious—it is Venice . . . romantic, randy Venice . . ." His voice rang out:

> "Once did She hold the gorgeous East in fee;
> And was the safeguard of the West: the worth
> Of Venice did not fall below her birth,
> Venice, the eldest Child of Liberty."

He paused.

"Byron," he added.

"Wordsworth," snapped Emma.

Brock ignored that.

"I am standing, actually standing in the Piazza San Marco, Venice. What is that building over there?"

"The Doge's Palace," said Emma.

"What? Where Othello stands before the Council in Act One?"

"Yes."

> "Most potent, grave, and reverend signiors,
> My very noble and approved good masters, . . ."

Brock swept the Doge and his Council a deep bow, and then allowed Emma to lead him away. She steered him along the Mercerie, over a small canal and across a deserted square. He was walking very slowly now, muttering to himself. His shoulders were hunched and his feet were beginning to shuffle. She glanced at him sharply. Was he drunk after one cognac? No, he was just turning himself into Shylock. They came to a little covered bridge over a canal and Emma walked up the dark steps with Brock following.

He was whining:

> "Signior Antonio, many a time and oft,
> In the Rialto you have rated me
> About my money and my usances:

> Still have I borne it with a patient shrug;
> For sufferance is the badge of all our tribe: . . ."

As he gave a patient shrug, Shylock missed his footing and collapsed on the ground in a flurry of Anglo-Saxon.

"Bloody stupid little bridge," said Brock, picking himself up. "What is it—the Bridge of Sighs?"

"No. It's the Rialto," said Emma sweetly.

And at that, even Brock Berowne was silent.

3

"No, no, no, Frank, I am not paying hotel bills for Brock Berowne just because the goddam Rome office screwed things up and got him here early!"

Karl and Walther were in the Production Office at the Palazzo Pavone, and Karl was shouting at Frank Jones, the Production Manager.

"Brock can get up off his ass and go back to London until I'm good and ready for him."

"But, Karl, that means paying his airfare twice over," said Frank Jones. "It'll cost more than his hotel bill."

"Fog," said Walther solemnly. "You remember—Sherlock Holmes, Charles Dickens. They get a lot of fog in England. Their planes get delayed. If Brock goes back, you can't be sure of getting him here on time."

Frank Jones wondered how anybody could be as idiotic as Walther. Fog in England, indeed! Karl would probably explode.

But Karl was considering.

"Frank," he said, "Walther's right. Tell Brock he can stay— but he better not run up any heavy bills or he'll pay them himself. OK, Walther?"

"*Aber ja, Herr Kapitän,*" said Walther. And he laughed.

Frank Jones suddenly realized that even Walther Meister had his good points. He telephoned Brock at his hotel and told him to spend a few days amusing himself in Venice, but not to spend any money. He didn't explain how Brock was to do one without the other. Brock mooched around the Piazza San Marco, the Piazzetta and the Rialto, but they were full of tourists, which bored him, so he drifted to the film set, where at least he could get free lunches and coffee.

"Emma, what's the name of this place?" he asked.

"Palazzo Pavone," said Emma. "That's the family crest over the doorway—it's terribly battered, but you can still just make out the shape of the peacock."

"Angels and ministers of grace defend us!" said Brock. "My God, if I'd known there was a peacock over that door I'd never have come in here, I'd have gone straight back home to London."

"But, Brock," said Emma, *"pavone* means 'peacock.' And anyway, what's wrong with a peacock? It's a beautiful creature."

"Peacocks mean bad luck for actors," said Brock. "It may be all right for other people, Emma, but believe me, as far as actors are concerned, the peacock means death."

He pulled a small grey object from his pocket and stroked it over and over again.

"My lucky hare's foot," he explained.

The hare's foot was old and almost bare of fur, with a few scarlet threads clinging to it, showing that once there had been a red ribbon tied round it.

"Emma darling," said Brock, "get me some garlic, for God's sake—and quickly. It keeps away the forces of evil."

It sounded ridiculous to Emma, but she asked Marco to get some garlic for Brock. Marco ran off, and Emma saw that Brock had gone over to Richard Traherne and was talking to him earnestly. Oh Lord, she thought, Richard will only laugh at him. But Richard reached inside his velvet tunic and pulled out a hare's foot, almost as battered and shapeless as the one belonging to Brock. He rubbed it several times and then slipped it back inside his tunic. So Richard too believed that the peacock was a bird of ill omen for an actor.

Marco came running back with a clove of garlic. Emma saw Brock offer some of it to Richard, who smiled and shook his head. Brock put all the garlic into his own pocket. Emma had a feeling that Brock was soon going to find himself very unpopular.

When work resumed after the break, Brock remained at the back of the set. He was recovering his self-confidence, but he was not happy. Watching other people make a film bored him, and there was absolutely nothing for him to do.

"Othello's occupation gone," he muttered.

Then he made the acquaintance of some of the pretty girls among the extras. Stephen was a little shocked. He thought Brock was a dirty old man. Brock was thirty-five, and thought of himself as in the prime of life. The girls certainly seemed to think so. And they didn't seem to notice the garlic.

At lunch-break Hal, Marco and Stephen gathered as usual around Emma's desk. Dave and Johnny, the two leading stunt men, joined them. Dave was big, dark and hatchet-faced, with a villainous scar down one cheek. Johnny was smaller, with fair hair and a beard. They were both wearing black leather costumes, and Stephen thought they looked very intimidating.

"Hal," said Dave, "who's this chap Leonidas what's-his-name who's playing Richard's sidekick?"

"Walther engaged him," said Hal.

There was a groan from the two stunt men.

"D'you know where Walther found him, smatterafact?" asked Johnny.

"I can tell you that," said Marco. "Mr. Walther was attending an international athletics meeting in the company of a pretty Greek lady, and Leonidas won a medal, and the Greek lady was very happy because he is her compatriot. She introduced Leonidas to Mr. Walther, and Mr. Walther offered him a contract on the spot—"

"Does Leonidas know anything about filming?" asked Dave. "You know what I mean . . ."

"—and he got married a few weeks ago," finished Marco.

"What!" said Hal.

Marco smiled. "Leonidas had only known her a few days,

but when you see her you will understand. His wife is a very lovely lady, and her name is Ariadne."

"Where is he now?" asked Hal.

"I do not know," said Marco. "You see, I was in Venice for several weeks before the rest of you arrived here. I was looking after the Production Office—that is how I met Leonidas and Ariadne. But when Mr. Meister got here, he said he would not pay any S.O.B. actor's hotel bills until he was acting on the picture, so Leonidas and Ariadne went away for a honeymoon. I have not seen them since."

"He's on his honeymoon," said Dave heavily. "He knows nothing about filming. He sounds a right daisy. I hope he speaks English—you know what I mean . . ."

"I know a few words of Greek, smatterafact," said Johnny. "It's a crazy language. They say 'Nay' for 'Yes' and 'OK' for 'No.' And 'Thank you' sounds like—like 'eff' something—"

"*Evkharisto,*" said Marco.

"That's it!" said Johnny. "I remember now. 'Eff Harry's toe.' That's no language for a Christian . . ."

"Come on," said Dave. "We'd better go and talk to Richard and Yorky—we'll have to nurse Leonidas through his scenes, and we'll have to simplify some of the stunts to make sure he doesn't kill anybody, you know what I mean . . ."

Stephen was startled. He watched them go, and then he turned to Emma.

"Leonidas couldn't really k-kill anybody, c-could he?" he asked. "I mean, they're n-not real swords and things they use?"

"No," said Emma, "but if he's not experienced he could certainly hurt somebody very badly. You watch the stunt men rehearsing and you'll see that every stunt is worked out very carefully and then rehearsed, almost like a ballet. Stunt men are professionals, and the one thing they hate is working with amateurs, because amateurs are unpredictable, and it does sound as though the romantic Leonidas is an amateur."

"Leonidas what's-his-name?" said Frank Jones. "No sweat, Hal. He's having a costume fitting upstairs right now."

There was the usual hubbub in the courtyard as Karl prepared to shoot a fight sequence along the balustrade with Richard, Dave and Johnny. They were all in costume, although Richard had his hair in curlers and a drooping pink hairnet. Karl was having a row with František the cameraman while all around them the members of the unit went on with their jobs. The camera crew and sound crew were following the moves of the fight along the balustrade, two men from the Art Department were tugging at a large crimson curtain, and Props men were moving through the courtyard carrying torches, tureens, great pasties made of plaster, and a stuffed swan. On the upper floor, musicians were tuning their instruments, and a few extras were rehearsing a dance. Walther came wandering up to Emma's desk.

"Emma," he said, "I've had a wonderful idea for this fight sequence—see?"

He showed her the back of a crumpled envelope on which he had scribbled a few words and some rough drawings. It was utterly unintelligible. Emma made encouraging noises. Hal and Marco, coming towards her with their scripts under their arms, noticed Walther and came to a discreet halt. So did Stephen. Nobody wanted to hear about Walther's wonderful idea.

High on a gantry overlooking the balustrade, an electrician suddenly dropped a large lamp, which crashed down on to the floor with a deafening explosion and a shattering of glass. There was dead silence as everybody looked towards the crash, and then froze, looking upwards.

Richard's unknown sidekick, Leonidas, had chosen this moment to appear at the top of the staircase in full costume. A beautiful young man, with fair hair curling to his shoulders, Leonidas wore his plum-coloured tunic and hose as though it was his everyday wear. He might have stepped out of a painting by Botticelli. But it was not Leonidas that everyone was staring at. It was his wife, Ariadne.

She looked about seventeen, a small, exquisite girl in a blue summer dress. She had a heart-shaped face and huge dark brown eyes, and, at a time when short curls were the fashion, this lovely child had long, red-gold hair falling over her shoulders and down to her waist. This was the "lovely lady" that Marco had spoken of, Ariadne who had met and married Leonidas a few weeks ago.

Film crews are accustomed to beautiful people, and they are not easily impressed. But there was no doubt that everyone was looking up at Ariadne as she stood beside Leonidas, high above them at the top of the great staircase.

When the lamp exploded, Leonidas had flung his arms around her. Now he relaxed and slipped his arm through hers. There was total silence as they descended the staircase. When they reached the courtyard, Ariadne stood with downcast eyes and folded hands. She didn't do anything or say anything to attract attention. She didn't need to. Men turned their faces to her as plants turn towards the sun. And it wasn't just the men. Babs Hairdresser, Beth Wardrobe and Emma were looking at her too.

She's Melisande, thought Emma. She's Guinevere. She's Helen of Troy . . .

She glanced at Hal.

"Star quality?" she asked softly, and he nodded. They had both seen star quality before. Not all so-called stars have it, but the top ones, the ones who last, they have it. It isn't charm or sex-appeal or personality, though people who have star quality usually have all these things. It is—something extra. And it looked as though little Ariadne had it.

Brock was murmuring to himself, and Emma could just hear the words.

"Shall I compare thee to a summer's day?
Thou art more lovely and more temperate:
Rough winds do shake the darling buds of May,
And summer's lease hath all too short a date: . . ."

Hal was the first to come out of his trance.

"Wait till Stella sees her!" he muttered. Emma smiled, and Marco gave a mock groan. Hal barked a few short commands, and the unit returned to work. Marco went over and greeted Ariadne and Leonidas like old friends. Then he took them to Walther, who was seated behind the camera. The electrician replaced the lamp, somebody swept up the mass of broken glass, and Karl resumed his row with František.

Nobody but Emma noticed that Richard and Yorky, up by the balustrade, were staring down at Leonidas as though he were Banquo's ghost. It was not hard to guess how Richard was feeling. He had several scenes to play with Leonidas. Would this beautiful young man steal them from him? Was this the beginning of the end for Richard Traherne, that ageless juvenile?

Emma gave a little shiver.

If looks could kill, she thought, Leonidas was a dead man.

4

Under Hal's command the state of apparent confusion dissolved into a state of readiness for shooting. Leonidas and Ariadne sat quietly with Walther at the back of the set. All those people not immediately concerned with the shot, and there seemed to be a great many of them, drifted towards Ariadne.

Dave and Johnny, dressed in the black leather costumes of Brock's henchmen, appeared at the top of the staircase. Richard joined them. Wearing green and gold velvet, with his dark hair curling casually as though it had never known the indignity of curlers and a pink hairnet, he was incredibly handsome.

Richard's himself again, thought Emma; then she remembered that the line referred to Richard III, and once more she shivered.

"Quiet, please, we're shooting!" shouted Hal.

"Silenzio! Si gira!" shouted Marco.

"Turn over," said Karl.

The operator switched on the camera.

"Speed up!" called his assistant.

The clapper-board clacked.

"ACTION!" shouted Karl.

Richard backed his way through the masked revellers and leaped up on to the balustrade, slashing down at Dave and Johnny. They hesitated, and he jumped down behind a pillar. They lashed out, their blades striking sparks from the stone pillar, and then Richard was up again and running along the narrow edge of the balustrade. They came after him and, as Dave lunged forward, Richard hurled himself off the balustrade and caught at the great crimson curtain. For a split second he hung there, and the curtain (carefully designed by the Art Department for the purpose) began to tear, slowly at first and then faster and faster, ripping from top to bottom and taking him thirty feet down to safety in the courtyard below.

There was a scatter of applause, and Stephen was astonished to see Richard leaning over the balcony clapping his hands with the rest. Only then did he realize that it was Yorky, the stunt double, who had run along the top of the balustrade and slid down the curtain. Yet he was sure that it had been Richard fighting at the beginning of the shot. He took his problem to Emma.

"Richard did the first part of the fight," she said. "But when he ducked down behind the pillar, he *stayed* down. Yorky was already hiding there, and after Dave and Johnny hit the pillar with their swords, Yorky jumped out, ran along the balustrade and slid down the curtain. Now we'll take a shot of Richard at the foot of the curtain."

There was a pause while the camera was moved and the scene was lit. Richard dropped the last few feet down to the courtyard, the curtain swirling round him. As he landed, he paused and looked up in the direction of the balustrade. A dagger was hurled into shot, narrowly missing him, and then the camera panned and tracked with him as he ran to the canal doorway and disappeared into the darkness.

When shooting was over that evening, Leonidas and Ariadne went upstairs to the Wardrobe Department, and Walther paused at Emma's desk on his way out. Stephen, Marco and Hal were there, and all of them were watching Ariadne as she left the set.

"Isn't that one lovely little lady?" asked Walther.

Emma agreed.

"Star quality, huh?" said Walther.

Again Emma agreed.

"I tell you something, Emma," said Walther. "If that little lady had shown up a few weeks earlier she'd have been playing the lead in this film instead of Stella Camay. OK, so she's never been in front of a camera in her life. With star quality, that don't matter. Did you see the way everybody on the set reacted to her? *That*'s what matters. I'm thinking of having the Hack write in a small part for her, just to give her some experience. But I'd say that for little Ariadne, the sky is going to be the limit!"

Walther floated off the set on Cloud Nine, and Emma turned to Hal and Marco.

"Did you hear that!" she said.

"I hope," said Marco carefully, "that *Stella* does not hear it!"

Hal laughed.

"I don't think Stella need worry," he said. "Walther's talking through his hat as usual."

The next morning, Stephen walked up the stairs to the first floor and was surprised to discover that half the set had disappeared and had been replaced by stone-walled corridors and a heavy wooden door, and a balcony. Musicians, dancers and masked revellers stood about while the camera and sound crews got ready for the first shot. The lovely Ariadne sat with Walther behind the camera, and anyone who, like Stephen, had time to spare, stood and looked at the lovely Ariadne.

Then Stella Camay walked on to the set. She saw Ariadne's glorious red-gold hair, and she saw Ariadne's fan club hovering in the background. You can't have more than one Queen Bee in a hive, every old Queen Bee knows that. Stella prepared to sting.

"*Ciao,* Walther!" she said.

"Hi, Stella," said Walther. "I'd like to have you meet Ariadne Andros—Leo's wife."

"*Ciao!*" said Ariadne softly.

Stella turned and looked down at her, apparently noticing her for the first time. Her smile of welcome faded into a look of pity, but her voice rang out loud and clear.

"Oh, you poor child!" she said. "What a terrible red wig! It's perfectly hideous. Do take it off and tell them to give you something more becoming."

Stephen and the other members of Ariadne's fan club were shocked, but apparently Ariadne's English was not good enough for her to understand Stella's gibe, and her face expressed nothing but polite incomprehension. Stella sat down with her back to Ariadne, and called Beth Wardrobe, Babs Hairdresser and Charles Make-Up to her side. Her faithful courtiers, they petted and patted her, they held up mirrors, they removed non-existent threads from the immaculate dress, they handed her the golden mask to peep through, and they effectively screened Stella from Ariadne until it was time to start shooting the scene of the masked revels.

The camera turned, the clapper-board clacked, and Karl shouted, "Action!" Stella, warned of a plot to abduct her, slipped away from the revels and ran down a corridor, but her way was suddenly barred by Dave and Johnny, while a third villain, played by an Italian small-part actor, called to her to stop. She turned, her back against the door and screamed in terror. Richard and Leonidas leaped down from the balcony and ran to her rescue.

And here they struck a snag. Leonidas was an athlete, but he was not an actor. He found it difficult to walk through a rehearsal, and so put his full weight and energy into every move, which meant that the stunt men had to do the same in sheer self-defence. And Leonidas was unpredictable in his movements, performing some of his most dramatic actions just outside the range of the camera. The camera operator swore, Dave and Johnny tried to guess which way Leonidas would move next, and the Italian small-part actor became nervous and kept fluffing his one and only line, "Not so fast, my lady!" Nerves were taut, tempers were short. Stella snapped at everybody. But Richard Traherne had himself well in hand and behaved impeccably, patiently repeating his action and dialogue, and only occasionally glancing towards Yorky and raising his eyes heavenwards in mute and tolerant amusement.

Towards the end of the day it became clear that the scene would not be finished that day, but would have to be completed on the morrow. Hal murmured to Karl that the Italian small-part actor was only engaged for one day.

"If I shoot with him tomorrow, I'll have to give him another day's pay?" said Karl.

Hal nodded.

"I'll finish him today," said Karl. "Let Stella go home."

Hal caught Beth Wardrobe's eye and nodded to her to take Stella away. Charles Make-Up went with them.

"Stella's finished for today?" he asked quietly as he passed Hal, and Hal nodded. Charles gave a great sigh of relief, and Hal grinned.

But Stella was not quite finished.

As she left the set with Beth and Charles, she glanced back at Ariadne still sitting quietly beside Walther, her long hair falling down her back. Stella's voice floated clearly above the general chatter.

"My dears," she said, "give her a doll to carry, and she'd be a perfect child-whore for an old man to play with!"

She screamed with laughter, and then allowed a scarlet-faced Beth and Charles to hustle her up the stairs to the star dressing-room. Ariadne did not appear to understand, but there was no doubt that Walther did. Emma noticed that his normally pale face had turned deep red. But he controlled himself as a confused and tired Leonidas left the set and walked towards Ariadne.

"Great work, Leonidas!" called Walther. "You were great!"

Leonidas paused.

"Is all right?" he asked uncertainly.

"Very much all right," said Walther heartily.

Leonidas relaxed. His worried frown disappeared and he turned towards Ariadne. She had jumped up as he approached, and now she threw her arms around him and kissed him. Leonidas grabbed a chair and sat very close to her. They held hands, and looked at each other, oblivious of everyone else. Emma felt reassured. As far as Ariadne and Leonidas were concerned, Stella's sting was harmless. Thankfully, Emma gave her mind to her job again. The camera position was changed, the lighting was changed, and Karl rehearsed Richard "killing" the small-part actor. The whole scene was rehearsed, lit and shot in fifteen minutes. It was the end of the day's shooting.

As the lights went out, and the great doors of the courtyard were opened, the husky gondolier was revealed waiting with his boat at the Palazzo landing-stage. Stella, looking sweet and serene in a white silk pants suit, swept down the great staircase and across the courtyard. She stepped into the gondola and was carried away.

The next morning was quiet and peaceful. Leonidas was not on call, which was a relief in itself. And since Leonidas was not on call, Ariadne was not on the set, so Stella was once more the undisputed queen of the Palazzo Pavone, and could afford to be gracious. Karl was shooting Stella's close-ups for the masked revels and the abduction scene: Stella removing her mask, Stella smiling, Stella laughing, Stella replacing her mask, Stella reacting in fear to a whispered warning of abduction. Stella in the corridor, turning with her back against the door and reacting to the offscreen cry of "Not so fast, my lady!" Stella cowering at the door as the shadow of a man fell across her.

Stephen noticed that the man's shadow was in fact made by an electrician moving a small board in front of one of the lamps.

"What's happened to the m-man who played the v-villain yesterday?" he asked.

"He was only engaged for one day's work," said Emma. "Karl wouldn't want to give him another day's pay just to say one line offscreen and to cast a shadow over Stella. I shall read the line to Stella, and she'll react to that."

"B-but your voice! It w-won't sound anything l-like that Italian actor's!" said Stephen.

"Don't worry," said Emma. "The audience won't hear my voice. The editor will cut me out and replace me with the Italian actor."

Stephen watched as they shot the scene.

Karl nodded to Emma, and she called out, "Not so fast, my lady!" Stella turned and cowered back against the door, and the shadow fell across her face. But Stella's reaction was not convincing. They tried again and again, but there was no fear in her eyes.

As they were starting the sixth take, Emma felt a hand pressing gently on her shoulder. She glanced up and saw Brock standing beside her. This time, when Karl said, "Cue, Emma," it was Brock's voice that they heard, ice-cold and terrifying, as wicked as Richard III. "Not so fast, my lady!" came the voice of Brock Berowne, and Stella screamed in sudden terror. Then she was swallowed up in the black shadow.

Karl was happy.

The camera crew was happy.

Brock was happy—at last he was doing his job, even if strictly speaking it was the Italian small-part actor's job.

Only Emma was faintly troubled, because she could have sworn that Stella's scream of terror had been absolutely genuine.

Why should Brock's voice have frightened Stella?

5

It was a difficult day at the Palazzo Pavone.

It had begun normally enough. The construction crew had worked all through the night to have a new set ready in the undercroft, only to be told by Karl at eight in the morning that it was exactly the opposite of what he had asked for, and the Art Director had resigned on the spot. However, the set would not be required until the afternoon, and doubtless by that time somebody would have sorted things out.

Half an hour later Karl began rehearsing on the corridor set on the first floor. The scene was very simple, involving only Stella Camay and Leonidas. But as Stella came down from her dressing-room she noticed Ariadne on the set.

" 'Fasten your seat-belts, this is going to be a bumpy ride . . .' " murmured Emma to Hal, and he grinned.

"All About Eve," said Stephen a little smugly. "Bette Davis's line."

"Joseph L. Mankiewicz," said a voice behind them.

They turned. L. J. Hacker stood there, affronted.

"Joseph L. Mankiewicz, the script-writer, wrote the line you have just quoted. It was *his* line. Bette Davis merely delivered it."

He stalked away, having struck a blow for script-writers everywhere, and started the long walk up the stairs to his office-cupboard.

"Quiet, please!" called Hal. "Settle down. Rehearsal!"

"Silenzio! Prova!" called Marco.

They rehearsed the scene. Stella, waiting for the cue for action, stood beside Leonidas like a furious icicle. Leonidas tried so hard to do everything right that he did everything wrong. But at last the shot was completed, and they prepared for the next one. Stella said not a word to Leonidas, but she demanded constant attention from Beth Wardrobe and Charles Make-Up, and she snapped at Marco when he offered her a chair to sit on between shots. When she was in front of the camera she had a succession of tantrums which involved shifting everybody out of sight because they made her feel nervous. But somehow the scenes were rehearsed and shot, and at last Hal signalled to Beth and Charles to take Stella to her dressing-room. When she had gone there was a general feeling of relief.

It didn't last.

Karl had devised an immensely complicated panning and tracking shot as Dave and Johnny chased Richard through the masked revellers, who scattered and fell, or dived under tables for safety. They rehearsed the scene over and over again. František the cameraman darted about, now peering through the viewfinder of the camera, now signalling to an electrician to adjust a lamp. Karl cursed the actors and the crew, and they cursed him back, though only František did so out loud. It was a hot day. At last Hal called for the coffee break.

Karl and František went off to have a look at the new undercroft set. Hal called the camera crew and the stunt men together.

"While Karl's away," he said, "let's rehearse the damned thing slowly. Bob, you stop us when anything goes wrong for the camera. Yorky, will you double for Richard?"

They worked their way through the scene, slowly at first, and then faster and faster until actors and camera were moving at full speed. They had lost their chance of a coffee break, but it was worth it. They wiped away the sweat and prepared to give Karl a pleasant surprise.

Karl and František returned from the undercroft. Without waiting for a rehearsal, Karl announced that he had scrapped the complicated panning and tracking shot and would shoot the sequence in short sections.

The camera crew swore.

František had to re-light the scene.

The stunt men had to change their moves.

It was a hot day, and getting hotter.

Tempers were frayed.

Everybody snapped at everybody else.

Time went by.

One o'clock. Some of the unit began muttering about a lunch-break.

Two o'clock. Everybody was muttering about a lunch-break. Karl pushed on.

Hal grimly held the simmering unit together, dominating it with the look in his eyes and the sound of his voice.

Three o'clock. The sequence was completed. Karl turned away and prepared to line up the first shot of the next scene.

Hal stopped him. He was a very angry man.

"You'll have to stop now, Karl," he said. "The boys have kept going to complete the sequence for you. It's three o'clock. They must have a break."

Karl glared at him.

"I'm the boss of this goddam picture!" he shouted. "I'll say when we have a break and—"

Hal turned away.

"Lunch-break!" he called. "One hour."

His voice rose effortlessly above Karl's. Hal had learned to make his voice carry through a Force 10 gale on board a minesweeper. If it came to a shouting-match he could beat Karl any day.

The unit scattered. Everyone hurried down the stairs to the courtyard where the lunch-boxes were stacked.

Walther came on to the set clutching his script and a few loose typewritten pages. He picked his way carefully among the cables and camera tracks as Karl resumed his argument with Hal.

"Karl!" cried Walther. "I've got a great idea for a scene!"

Karl stopped arguing.

"Which scene, Walther?" he said.

"The one where Richard escapes from the two villains who were trying to abduct Stella—the scene among the masked revellers."

Stephen, standing beside Emma, intervened quickly, fearful of another outburst from Karl.

"B-but Mr. M-Meister has j-just shot that scene!" he said.

Emma kicked him sharply. He looked down at her in surprise. When he looked up again, Karl had his arm around Walther and was walking him away across the set in search of a quiet corner.

"Tell me about it, Walther," he said kindly.

"Stephen," called Hal, "come and give Marco a hand with the lunch-boxes, would you?"

Stephen did what he could. He and Marco handed out lunch-boxes to the grumbling, sweating members of the unit, who grabbed at the boxes and went off to find a corner of a staircase or some other perch where they could eat. Many of them were no longer hungry, but they were determined to eat, if only to spite the management. After the main crush was over, Emma went across and collected her lunch-box.

"Marco," said Hal, "tell Stella she's finished."

Marco turned quickly to look at him.

"Finished?" he said. "Stella—*finished?*"

"Finished for today," said Hal.

"Oh, I see," said Marco. "For a moment I thought—I mean, I remember what Mr. Walther said about Ariadne replacing her—"

He glanced awkwardly around in case he had been indiscreet.

"Don't worry," said Hal. "Nobody's put the skids under Stella Camay. She's quite safe."

"Would you l-like me to t-take a lunch-box to Stella, Marco?" said Stephen.

"Thank you, Stephen, but I have to tell her that she has finished shooting, so I will take her lunch-box. Also I have to take a lunch-box to Mr. Meister."

"D-don't forget M-Mr. Walther," said Stephen.

"Oh yes," said Marco. "I was not expecting Mr. Walther on the set today. OK, I take three lunch-boxes."

They watched idly as he collected the three lunch-boxes and walked up the staircase.

"He's a good chap," said Hal. "Gets on with the job. Never makes a fuss. More like an Englishman than a w——"

He caught Emma's eye and stopped. In silence they walked over to Emma's desk and began to eat.

Stephen looked around him with a worried expression. He dropped his voice.

"You know, this script is t-terrible!" he said.

"You should have seen the last one," said Hal drily.

"Isn't this the first one, then?" said Stephen.

"Lord, no," said Emma. "The story began life as a Western. In script number one there was a villainous sheriff, a prissy school-teacher and a cowboy hero, and after a lot of hassle and a spectacular rodeo, the cowboy shot the villain and married the school-teacher. In script number two it was the school-teacher who shot the villain, but otherwise the story was the same. In script number three the story was shifted to mediae-val England, in script number four it was set in Nuremberg with overtones of *The Meistersingers,* and by script number five it was set in Italy, and the rodeo was changed into the Palio of Siena—Karl's wife had seen the Palio and was just crazy about it. That's when the title was changed to *The Trumpets of Tuscany* —Karl's wife thought that sounded real neat. Mr. Hacker is now working on script number six . . ."

Marco returned.

"Stella wants to go off after lunch and visit one of the islands with her gondolier," he said. "I am going to tell him."

He went towards the canal. Emma picked up the empty lunch-boxes and returned them to the dump. It was time to get back to work.

The rest of the day passed quickly. They moved down to the undercroft which had been transformed into a vaulted cellar with a labyrinth of underground passages. After the open sky of the courtyard, the low ceiling of the undercroft was oppressive. Everybody was glad when six o'clock came and shooting ended.

Emma was packing up when Hal came towards her. Her shoulders drooped and her hair looked damp upon her forehead.

Poor Emma, he thought, you look as tired as I feel.

Aloud he said, "Emma, can you give Penny a hand with some typing tonight? Hacker's written a whole lot of new scenes and they have to go out to everyone this evening."

"Oh no!" said Emma. "Hal, I can't, I simply can't . . ."

Then she looked at him.

Poor Hal, she thought, you look as tired as I feel.

Aloud she said, "Oh, all right. Does Penny want to start right now?"

"No," said Hal. "Have your dinner first."

"OK," said Emma. "I'll have a look at the new scenes while I'm eating. But I warn you, I am not typing Walther's new rescue scene, however brilliant. The rescue scene is in the can, and that's the end of it."

After dinner, Emma returned to the Palazzo Pavone and the Production Office. Once it had been the porter's lodge. Now it contained a desk and telephone for the Production Manager, a desk and a large-carriage typewriter for the Production Secretary, a filing cabinet, a safe, a duplicator, an electric kettle, wall-charts, piles of scripts, stacks of coloured paper, boxes of stencils, a stray pair of shoes and a gondola cushion smelling of mould. Emma and Penny slogged away, typing the new pages, and then running off copies on coloured paper on the ancient and temperamental duplicator. Emma hated that duplicator. It had to be turned by hand like an old-fashioned gramophone, its supply of thick black ink needed a lot of messy topping up, and just when it seemed to be running smoothly at last, it would spit out a handful of pages with half the lines missing. But at last it was done.

"Right," said Penny. "Now we've got to check, collate and staple—oh, *ciao*, Marco!"

"I have to take all the copies round to the hotels as soon as they are ready," he said. "You look tired, Emma. Can I help?"

"I *am* tired, Marco," said Emma. "Bless you."

She was glad of the chance to escape from the stuffy little office, its atmosphere made all the worse by Penny's chain-smoking. She went outside to the cool air of the evening and walked slowly through the silent, shadowy courtyard. Surely, she thought, nothing is as empty as an empty film set. The tall gantries stood on guard along one wall, and her own small wooden desk was tucked away in the corner by the landing-stage doorway. Above the door glimmered the white stone shield with its weather-worn peacock. She smiled indulgently, thinking of Brock and his ridiculous fear of peacocks. Actors!

She stepped out on to the landing-stage and looked down at the dark canal. It was a gloomy scene, with black water lapping softly against the cold stone steps. The atmosphere was chilly and dank, and she gave a sudden little shiver.

A black gondola came gliding noiselessly towards her along the canal, a gondola with a small curtained cabin amidships. She watched dreamily as the boat approached, and then she recognized the boatman as Stella's husky gondolier, bringing his boat in to the landing-stage where Emma was standing.

She withdrew into the shadows. She didn't want to watch Stella Camay and the gondolier making their farewells. But as she turned to go into the courtyard, her skirt caught on a hook in the wall, and she had to pause to free it. So she saw the gondola glide silently to the Palazzo steps, saw the gondolier tap gently on the roof of the cabin below him, saw him open the curtains—and then saw him turn a mute and horrified face, pale in the reflected light of the boat's swinging lantern.

Emma ran back through the courtyard and found Marco leaving the Production Office with an armful of the new script pages.

"Marco," she said quietly, "please come quickly. It's Stella. Her gondola's here and—something's wrong."

Marco dropped the scripts and hurried out to the landing-stage. The gondolier was looking down at the pale figure of Stella lying in the darkness of the little cabin. He looked up fearfully as Marco called softly to him.

Marco jumped down into the gondola and bent over Stella. He felt her pulse, her heart. He drew back, and stepped ashore to where Emma was waiting.

"I think Stella is dead," he said. "I will ring the company doctor—I do not think there is anything he can do for her, but he will have to see her."

"I'll call him," said Emma. "You'd better stay with the gondolier and—and with Stella. And I'd better call Hal. And then—"

"And then somebody will have to tell Karl," said Marco.

"Hal's job," said Emma.

But when she rang him, Hal was not at his hotel, so it was Emma who rang Karl and broke the news to him that Stella Camay was dead.

A few minutes later she stepped into the courtyard to find that the moon had come out from behind the clouds and was lighting up the whole of the Palazzo with sudden brilliance. The tall black skeletons of the gantries threw spidery shadows across the floor, and the pale stone arches of the balustrade floated, white as bone, above the darkness of the undercroft. Emma glanced towards the canal doorway, where she could see Marco and the gondolier standing motionless looking down at Stella. Above the doorway, clear and sharp in the moonlight, was the stone shield with the proud device of the peacock.

6

Half an hour later Karl came storming into the office where Marco, Emma and Penny sat quietly drinking coffee out of cardboard cups. The gondolier sat hunched on a pile of boxes of duplicating paper, his face in his hands, sobbing noisily. The company doctor had given him a sedative, but so far it hadn't worked.

The doctor was pouring coffee for himself, and he offered the cup to Karl, who brushed it aside.

"Is Stella on call tomorrow?" he asked.

"No," said Marco, Emma and Penny together. It had been one of the first things they had thought of. Callous? Yes. Professional? Yes to that too.

"Stella had no more scenes here in Venice—her next scenes were all at La Rocca," said Emma.

"We move there next week. Well, we better get a replacement for her," said Karl, as though Stella had been no more than a piece of furniture that had regrettably been broken.

The doctor looked unhappy.

"Are you proposing to carry on filming?" he asked.

"Why not?" barked Karl.

"Because," said the doctor, "I fear this is a matter for the police. I cannot commit myself, of course, but I do not think that Stella Camay died from natural causes."

Karl stared at him, then slowly raised a questioning eyebrow.

"I think," said the doctor, very carefully and very softly, "I think that Stella Camay was poisoned."

Karl was shocked into silence.

For a while the only sound in the office was the sobbing of the gondolier. At last Karl turned to Marco.

"Call the police," he said heavily. "The sooner they get here and take her away the better."

Commissario Gabrieli and his assistant Calvi arrived at the Palazzo Pavone with the Examining Magistrate. They sealed Stella's dressing-room and then, while the police doctor, photographer and fingerprint expert did their work outside in the gondola, the Examining Magistrate questioned Marco, Emma and Penny, and Commissario Gabrieli questioned the gondolier.

"When she gets into the boat the lady is well, very well, though I think perhaps she has had a little too much wine with her lunch. I take her to an island—we had been there many times recently—she calls it 'her' island—and when we get there we drink some wine—"

"Both of you drank the wine?" asked Gabrieli.

"Yes."

"Where did you get the wine?"

"The lady brought it with her."

"Glasses?"

"We drink from the bottle."

"Right—so you both drank some wine. Then?"

"We make love. Then the lady drinks some more wine, and goes to sleep. Suddenly the lady is sick, very sick. She has pains, cramps, much anguish. Then she becomes more comfortable. I lift her into the boat and return quickly to the Palazzo here."

"She was still alive when you put her into the boat to return home?"

The man looked horrified.

"Oh yes, yes! I think if I can just get her home to her friends here they will call a doctor, and he will make her well—never do I row so fast as I row tonight to bring the lady home. But when I get here, Signor Marco looks at her and tells me she is dead."

The police doctor came into the office and Gabrieli looked at him.

"I'll have to do a proper investigation," said the doctor, "but at the moment it looks like straightforward poisoning. Probably taken with food or drink."

She had some wine to drink on the island," said Gabrieli.

"See if you can get hold of the bottle," said the doctor. "The contents will have to be analysed."

"No sign of a bottle in the gondola," said Calvi.

Gabrieli turned to the gondolier.

"The bottle of wine—what happened to it?"

The gondolier stared at him stupidly.

"I don't know . . . I left it on the island . . . but there wasn't much left . . ."

Gabrieli spoke to the Examining Magistrate.

"With your permission," he said, "I think we should get out to the island straight away."

It was three in the morning when the police launch approached the island. A thick fog had rolled over the lagoon, and foghorns boomed and wailed in the ghostly whiteness. Gaunt black treetrunks marking the channels rose up through the water like bony fingers. Dark shapes loomed up out of the pale, dank mist, and then sank back as the launch sped past.

"There it is!" said the gondolier suddenly. "That's the island!"

The launch's searchlights picked out the high blank walls of a ruined and roofless abbey soaring skywards into the fog. The launch slowed down and came gently in to land, stirring up a thick batter of seaweed. The engine stopped, and in the sudden silence they stepped ashore, slipping on the wet algae, bright green in the launch's powerful lights.

It was a desolate place, smelling of damp, and decay, and

rottenness. The three men picked their way carefully past shallow, scummy pools, filled with empty tins, bits of broken plastic, and the detritus of the lagoon. Small animals scuttled and darted away beneath their feet.

Dear God! thought Gabrieli. What a place to bring a woman!

He followed the gondolier as he led them past the outside of the old abbey and turned into the shelter of a wall.

"Here?" said Gabrieli.

The gondolier seemed to sense some criticism of his choice of venue.

"I bring cushions for her from the gondola," he said sullenly. "She is very comfortable . . ."

"And where did you leave the wine-bottle?"

"About here somewhere," said the gondolier. "But the wine won't be worth drinking . . ."

Gabrieli and Calvi swung their torches over the rough ground.

"Is this it?" asked Calvi.

He pointed to a bottle half-floating in a puddle of slime and seaweed.

"Yes," said the gondolier, and stooped to pick it up.

"Don't touch it!" snapped Calvi.

The gondolier drew back, and then watched uncomprehendingly as Calvi slipped a plastic bag over the neck of the bottle and pulled it out of the puddle.

"Right," said Gabrieli. "Cover the area with a plastic sheet —Gino and his boys can have the pleasure of coming out here in daylight and collecting samples for analysis. We can go home now."

At the Palazzo Pavone the press had a field day. Photographers swarmed around taking pictures of everybody going in or out. Then they went along the canal and took pictures of "the fatal gondola"—it was not the actual boat in which Stella had died, because that was in the hands of the police, but one gondola looks very much like another in a newspaper photograph, and several enterprising gondoliers were quick to profit from this unexpected demand for their services. Then the press lost interest, for Elizabeth Taylor arrived in Rome and swept Stella Camay into oblivion.

"The doctor says it was arsenic," said Gabrieli. He and Calvi were back in the office at the Questura.

"Powdered arsenic? Stuff that looks like sugar?" said Calvi.

"Most likely," said Gabrieli. "She swallowed it, drank a lot of wine, went out to the island, drank some more wine, was very sick and suffered painful cramps. Became more comfortable, was helped into the boat and died on the way home. We'll have to find out what she had to eat and drink—"

"I've got the lab report on the bottle from the island," said Calvi. "They say it's clean."

"Clean!" muttered Gabrieli, recalling the place where the bottle had been found.

"Well, no trace of arsenic, anyway," amended Calvi.

"So it must have been something she ate or drank before she went out to the island."

"Yes."

"Right—back to the Palazzo Pavone. Have a talk to the woman who cleans Stella Camay's dressing-room."

Giovanna the cleaning lady was stout, respectable, diligent and voluble. The signora had gone out, leaving a lot of soiled tissues, an empty lunch-box and an empty wine-bottle, all of which Giovanna had thrown away. It was no more than Calvi expected, but all the same he cursed Giovanna's zeal. No chance now of establishing exactly how Stella Camay had taken the arsenic.

Had Giovanna noticed any white powder?

White powder? White powder? Giovanna's voice went up an octave. Of *course* there was white powder! The signora scattered face powder all over the dressing-table, all over the floor, for Giovanna to clear up. Calvi had to wait for Giovanna to cool down. Clearly the face powder was a sore point with her.

What about sugar? Did she keep any white sugar for the signora to take with her coffee?

Giovanna flung open the door of a small white cupboard. Neat packets of cube sugar were piled in a shining blue china bowl beside some cups and saucers. Calvi emptied the contents of the bowl into a plastic bag, although he had little hope that there would be anything but sugar inside those tightly closed packets. Then he sealed up the dressing-room again and walked down the stairs to the Production Office.

The day's supply of lunch-boxes had just arrived, and Penny was stacking them on the big table near the office. Calvi looked at them.

"Is that the kind of lunch-box that Stella Camay would have had?" he asked, and Penny nodded. "She didn't have anything special?"

"No," said Penny. "We all have exactly the same—Karl Meister, Stella Camay, everybody on the unit."

"I would like to take one as a sample," said Calvi.

Penny presented him with a lunch-box, and Calvi returned to the Questura.

"The cleaner had thrown away Stella Camay's lunch-box and wine-bottle," he said. "There were some wrapped sugar cubes, which I don't think could possibly have contained poison—"

He showed them to Gabrieli.

"I agree," said Gabrieli. "But all the same they had better be analysed. What's in the box?"

"It's one of the lunch-boxes that was delivered to the Palazzo today. The kind of thing Stella Camay would have had. They all have the same, so I thought we ought to have one as a sample."

As Calvi spoke, he opened the lunch-box. They looked at the food tucked into the neat little compartments. Pasta, ham, fruit, cheese—and a piece of pastry half smothered in loose white sugar.

They looked at the pastry. They looked at each other.

"Ring the Production Office," said Gabrieli. "Find out who supplies their lunch-boxes. Then ring the supplier and find out exactly what was in the lunch-boxes on the day that Stella Camay died. If there was pastry with sugar I think we know how the arsenic was administered."

Hal, Emma and Stephen were eating their lunch at Emma's desk in the Palazzo courtyard, surrounded by the usual picnickers.

"Penny says that the Detective Calvi took away one of the lunch-boxes this morning, and then later he rang up to ask for the name of the suppliers," said Emma.

"He seems to think the arsenic was in Stella's lunch-box," said Hal.

"I thought arsenic w-was the stuff they put in w-weed-killer or rat-poison, or something—surely it would look n-nasty?" said Stephen, picking the pastry out of his box and scattering sugar all over his script.

"It's a white powder," said Hal. "I suppose it could be mixed with sugar—"

He broke off, staring at Stephen who was dabbing up the spilt sugar on his moistened fingers. Emma followed his gaze.

"Don't you remember?" she said excitedly. "That's exactly what Stella did—you know—when she helped herself to Stephen's pastry—"

"I'd been saving it for the l-last," said Stephen, still resentful.

"—and she spilt the sugar and licked her fingers and sucked all the sugar off them! We all do it every day. Do you think that's how it happened?"

"Arsenic—mixed with the sugar on her pastry?" said Hal.

Stephen said nothing, but he quietly put his uneaten pastry to one side and carefully wiped every trace of sugar off his fingers.

"The suppliers confirm that there was pastry with sugar," said Gabrieli. "So the arsenic must have been in the lunch-box. Who gave it to her?"

Calvi checked his notebook.

"The Assistant Director Marco took it to her dressing-room."

"Call him in," said Gabrieli grimly.

Emma was indignant.

"But they can't suspect *Marco* of poisoning Stella!" she exclaimed.

Hal said reluctantly, "Well, he did give the lunch-box to her."

"He only *carried* the box!" said Emma angrily. "He wasn't responsible for whatever was inside it. I carry a script about all day, but I'm not responsible for the rubbish inside it!"

Too late she noticed the small, stiff figure of L. J. Hacker stalking away, offended, just like the Ghost in Hamlet.

"Let us go through it again," said Commissario Gabrieli. "You took the lunch-box to Signora Camay—where was it when you picked it up?"

"It was with a whole lot of other lunch-boxes on the table," said Marco.

"You actually picked it up? Nobody else picked it up and gave it to you?"

"No. I picked it up myself."

"Did you pick up any other boxes?"

Marco thought for a moment.

"Yes," he said. "I picked up two boxes from the table. One for Stella Camay, and one for Mr. Walther—he had arrived on the set unexpectedly. Normally I'd have set a box aside for him, like Mr. Meister's."

"Mr. Meister's?" queried Gabrieli.

"I always used to put one box aside for him, and one for Mr. Walther if he was expected. I used to put the boxes on a ledge beside the Production Office, and then whenever there was a break, I'd slip upstairs with them and leave them ready for Mr. Meister and Mr. Walther in their offices."

"And on this day—when did you take the boxes upstairs?"

"There was no chance of a break. Mr. Meister was filming a very difficult sequence, and he insisted on going on and on, long after we should have broken for lunch—we didn't stop until three o'clock, and we were all very tired and irritable—"

"So you picked up *three* lunch-boxes—one from the ledge and two from the table. Was there any way of knowing which was which?"

Marco tried to visualize them.

"No," he said. "They looked exactly alike. I took all three boxes into Mr. Meister's office—left one on his desk—then into Mr. Walther's office and left one on *his* desk—and took the third one to Stella."

"Which box was on top?"

"I don't know," said Marco. "I expect I put the top one on Mr. Meister's desk, and the middle one on Mr. Walther's, and then took the last one to Stella. But I don't know."

"Was anybody in either of the offices?"

"No—Mr. Meister and his cousin were discussing a scene downstairs for quite a long time."

"You say you had one lunch-box set aside on the ledge for Mr. Meister. How long was it there?"

"I don't know," said Marco. "But at least four, perhaps five hours."

"Did anybody know about the lunch-box being put aside for Mr. Meister?"

"I suppose—quite a lot of people knew," said Marco. "There was no secret about it. It happened every day."

"Did Mr. Walther know about it?"

"I think he did," said Marco slowly. "Yes—I remember— there was one day when he collected the two boxes off the ledge himself. Didn't think to tell me, of course, and then when I rushed upstairs with two more lunch-boxes, I found him already eating. Mr. Walther thought it was very funny."

"Could somebody have tampered with the box while it was on the ledge?"

"I don't think so. It's in a dark part of the set, and somebody might see you—people are always passing."

"Could somebody have removed the box, and substituted another one—one which already contained poisoned food?" asked Gabrieli.

"If you had a box already poisoned—then, yes, I think you could switch the boxes quite easily without fear of discovery, provided you chose a time when everybody on the set was very busy."

"And everybody on the set was pretty busy that day?" asked Gabrieli.

"Yes," said Marco. "Everybody was very busy."

7

"B-but surely we can d-do *something?*" said Stephen.

It was lunch-time at the Palazzo Pavone. Marco had returned from the Questura and was sitting with Hal and Stephen at Emma's desk.

"Like what?" said Hal. "Turn ourselves into a bunch of amateur detectives? We'd be useless. Leave that to the professionals. Our job is to get on and make the film."

"B-but surely if we all p-put our heads together," said Stephen, "we c-could think of some *reason* for it—something the p-police might not know—just to g-give them a lead. I m-mean, it all seems so senseless—why should anybody want to k-kill Stella?"

"I have just read a piece about Stella in one of the weekly magazines," said Marco, "which suggests a reason—a very unpleasant one. They are suggesting that her death was some kind of revenge killing because she betrayed somebody in the war."

"Oh—no!" said Stephen, pained.

"Have they any facts to go on?" asked Emma.

"If they have, they do not produce them," said Marco. "Only that her early life is obscure, and she changed her name —silly things like that. I suppose it is just to make a scandal—it helps to sell more copies of their magazine."

"Plenty of old scores to be settled," said Hal slowly. "It must have been difficult to know who you could trust. It was different in England. We didn't have the enemy living among us."

Emma said, "I'd forgotten that the war ended less than ten

years ago. It seems a long time. But if you or your family or your friends had been betrayed, and you suddenly met the person who did it—"

"Mr. Walther said that Leonidas's family played a big part in the Greek Resistance," said Marco.

"František was in Czechoslovakia when war broke out," said Emma. "He escaped to England and fought with the Free Czechs—"

"Karl Meister was an officer in the US Army," said Stephen. "We had an information sheet about him at our film society. He was in Europe with the O.S.S.—they had a network of secret agents and that sort of thing—"

"Stop that!" said Hal sharply. "It's the very thing we must *not* do! Everybody will suspect everybody else. The whole damned unit will become hysterical!"

"But supposing the k-killer strikes again?" asked Stephen.

"Oh, stop talking like a B picture!" snapped Hal. "Suppose we discover it's somebody important to the film—"

"Yes," said Emma uncomfortably, "I suppose it is most likely to be somebody on the unit—"

"You'd wreck the film," said Hal. "Throw a hundred people out of work. You won't bring Stella back."

"But it's m-murder!" cried Stephen. "I'm sorry about the f-film, and the p-people out of work—b-but human life must come f-first!"

"People who work in films get sick, like anybody else," said Hal. "They have accidents. They die from natural causes. We're used to that. It's like an army going into battle. Some-body's knocked out. You close ranks and carry on."

"Natural c-causes, yes," said Stephen. "B-but Stella didn't d-die from natural causes. This is d-different. This is m-murder—and we ought to d-do something about it. Stella's d-dead, and nobody c-cares! K-Karl will just write her out of the f-film and write somebody else in. The Queen is d-dead, l-long live the Queen!"

His voice cracked. He jumped to his feet and ran away

through the crowded courtyard. Emma glanced at Hal. He nodded, and she hurried after Stephen.

"I am sorry, Hal," said Marco. "It was my fault—I should not have spoken about the magazine article."

"Don't do it again," said Hal. "Might open old wounds."

"I have already done so," said Marco. He hesitated, and then said, "You were right about not knowing who you could trust during the war—I found that out." He took a deep breath, and then said tonelessly, "My family was what you would call 'on the wrong side.' My father supported Mussolini."

"A lot of English people admired him before the war," said Hal. "Didn't agree with them myself—"

"My father did not *admire* Mussolini!" Marco seemed shocked at the idea. "My father belonged to a very old family. He regarded Mussolini as a peasant. But I remember my father saying—I was only a boy at the time, of course—I remember my father saying he would not invite Mussolini to dine at our house, but he would be proud to die for him."

"And did he?"

"Die for Mussolini? I do not know. He died, yes. But for Mussolini, for Italy, for some crazy notion of honour—I do not *know* why." Marco's voice quavered and tailed away. Then he burst out angrily, "And what about his family and his friends? Did they die with him? No! They were too busy turning their coats. When my mother died, soon after my father, I turned to them for help. They called me a Fascist bastard and kicked me out!"

There was a pause.

"When they interviewed you at the Questura," said Hal, "did they know your background?"

"Of course," said Marco, surprised. "My family name is on my papers."

"Was it—tough, the questioning?"

Marco considered.

"It was—thorough," he said.

"You weren't hurt? Physically ill-treated?"

"No, no, only my pride was hurt. But that can be harder to bear than mere physical pain."

"Your pride was hurt because they suspected you of murdering Stella?"

"No." Marco flushed. "My pride was hurt because I had to admit to the Commissario—who is only a policeman—that a man of my family was carrying lunch-boxes, like a servant."

Hal stared at him.

"It is *la bella figura,* you know," said Marco, and forced a smile. "I think you call it 'cutting a good figure.' It is so very important to an Italian."

"Why didn't you tell me so?" asked Hal. "Somebody else could have carried the lunch-boxes."

Marco was silent.

"We leave for La Rocca at the end of the week," said Hal. "Do you want me to get someone else to look after the lunch-boxes till then?"

"That is good of you, Hal," said Marco, "but no, I think it is better if I continue looking after the lunch-boxes for Mr. Meister and Mr. Walther, otherwise—"

"Otherwise people might think I didn't trust you, eh?" said Hal. "Isn't that *la bella figura* again?"

"Yes, I suppose it is," said Marco, and he laughed at the sheer absurdity of it all.

Hal was relieved. Marco's outburst had worried him. He reminded himself that Marco had not only had to endure a "thorough" questioning by Commissario Gabrieli, but he had also been coping with the stress of working for Karl Meister, who had been known to overwhelm men much older than Marco. Good lad, he thought.

Aloud he said, "If we're going to leave for La Rocca at the end of the week, somebody is going to have to replace Stella Camay a bit sharpish."

Somebody was going to have to replace Stella Camay—but who? There were plenty of candidates. Every post brought sacks of letters and photographs of beautiful girls. Few were glanced at, and none was acknowledged. In the Production Office, transatlantic cables arrived daily from the studios in Hollywood, sending Karl the names and vital statistics of actresses who might replace Stella Camay.

"Penny, what does Karl say about the latest suggestions?" asked Frank Jones, the Production Manager.

"Karl says," said Penny, "and I quote—'Miss A is box-office poison, Miss B is too expensive, Miss C has a mouth like an alligator, Miss D is rotten with the pox and I wouldn't have her within a mile of me . . .' End quote."

Emma was working with Karl in his office when Walther came in.

"Karl," he said, "I have found you a replacement for Stella."

Karl raised one eyebrow.

"Ariadne?" he said. "No experience."

"Star quality," said Walther. "And she'd be cheaper than any of the studio broads."

"I don't give a damn about the money!" said Karl, with such feeling that for a moment Emma almost believed him. "But— could she do it?"

"Give her a test and find out," said Walther.

"OK," said Karl suddenly. "We'll run some tests with her." He thought for a moment. "The big difference between Stella and Ariadne is the colour of their hair, but for the scenes at the revels Stella's hair was hidden by her head-dress—right, Emma?"

Emma nodded. She could guess what was coming.

"We can re-take all Stella's close shots with Ariadne in the same costume and head-dress. If the tests are any good, we can just cut Stella out and slot Ariadne in . . . OK, Walther?"

"Aber ja, Herr Kapitän," said Walther. And he laughed.

So the next evening, after a full day's work at the Palazzo Pavone, the unit stayed late to shoot tests of Ariadne. She looked lovely in Stella's costume, but Gerry the Sound Recordist reported sadly that her lines were unintelligible.

"Her accent's as thick as a club sandwich," he said.

"Let's hear it," said Karl.

He put on the headphones as Gerry played back the recording. Around him was the usual buzz of conversation. Karl shook his head impatiently.

"Let's have quiet, Hal," he called.

"Quiet, everybody!" shouted Hal.

"Silenzio!" shouted Marco.

The unit quietened down to half its normal volume.

"I can't hear properly on these goddam cans of yours, Gerry," said Karl. "Let's hear her on playback."

As Ariadne's fresh young voice came fluting over the playback the unit quietened down to complete silence.

"Oh, veeda lees dee spud?" asked Ariadne, adding, "To sigh soot, eye yama V R E."

The Italian members of the crew thought it sounded very pretty.

"What in hell's she supposed to be saying?" growled Karl. "Emma, gimme the lines."

" 'Oh, whither leads this path?' " said Emma. " 'To say sooth, I am a-weary.' "

Karl thought for a moment.

"We better have the Hack re-write all Ariadne's lines. Emma can help him—she'll know which words Ariadne can pronounce and which she can't."

It was nearly midnight when a very tired Emma met Hacker in the tiny bar of his hotel.

"What was the line?" he asked.

" 'Oh, whither leads this path? To say sooth, I am

a-weary,' " said Emma with feeling. "She pronounced it just like an Italian."

"I thought she was Greek," said Hacker.

"So did I," said Emma. "But her accent is quite definitely Italian. I think perhaps she's only Greek by marriage."

"I certainly would not expect a Greek to have trouble with the 'th' sound," said Hacker. "Lots of our Greek-based words have 'th' in them. Theatre—thrombosis—theology—"

"Theology!" cried Emma. "Good Lord, I've just realized— theology—theos—Zeus—Deus—Dio—Dieu—they're all the same word for God! And I've never seen it till now. Oh, I do *love* words!"

Her tiredness slipped from her and her eyes shone.

"Do you think 'Tuesday' is a 'theos' word too?" she asked.

"Temper your enthusiasm with a modicum of restraint," said Hacker. It was the first time Emma had ever seen him smile. He looked a different man altogether. "Though if you're so interested in etymology you might like to look up 'enthusiasm' some time—that's a 'theos' word too. I must say I'm not surprised Ariadne had trouble—most of the lines in this picture are dreadfully unspeakable and unspeakably dreadful."

He paused, and Emma wondered if he was hoping for a round of applause.

"I hope you don't think *I* wrote this ineffable rubbish," he said. "I've merely inherited it from the writers of earlier scripts. Karl sees nothing wrong with it. He's so utterly insensitive to the English language I could kill him. Ah well, if all this means that I'm going to have a chance to write some good, plain English, then Stella did not die in vain."

His choice of words struck Emma as unfortunate.

Later in the week, Karl called for a whole day and evening to be devoted to Ariadne's tests, complete with Hacker's new dialogue. He began with the scene where the young princess thanked the stranger for saving her life, a scene which gradually blossomed into a love-duet. Richard Traherne played up to her very well, but when the scene was over Karl did not ask him to stay on and feed the offscreen lines to Ariadne for her close-ups. So Richard went home, and it was Brock who spoke the offscreen lines, Brock reeking of garlic and clutching his lucky hare's foot, which by now had lost the last vestiges of fur and was nothing but a smooth piece of bone. Then Karl called for close-ups of Ariadne at the masked revels. She went through all the reactions as Stella had done, including the terrified scream at Brock's offscreen whisper, "Not so fast, my lady!" As soon as the scene was completed, Brock too went home. He was uneasy in the Peacock Palace, and was glad to get away.

"OK," said Karl. "Now the scene in the gondola."

It was ten o'clock at night, and there was some muttering, but it was the last of the tests and the weary crew lashed the camera boat to the stern of the gondola. Karl, Emma and the camera crew squashed into the boat with the camera. Ariadne stepped into the gondola. She took up Stella's position, reclining on the silken cushions, playing with the gilded mask, smiling, or looking pensive.

When it came to the big close-up, Ernie was about to slip the flattering filter before the lens when Karl stopped him.

"Let's see how she looks without that," he said. "We better know the worst."

Emma crouched on her hands and knees in the bottom of the boat as Karl, standing behind her, leaned over her and gave Ariadne her instructions.

"I want you to close your eyes, Ariadne," he said softly. "And when I tell you to open them, I want you to look straight at the camera and think about—"

He paused. It was one thing to tell Stella Camay to think about Love. It was her stock-in-trade. Clearly Karl felt a little delicacy in dealing with Ariadne.

"Look straight at the camera, Ariadne," he said, "and think about—Leonidas . . ."

Emma, crouched down in the boat with Karl leaning over her, could not see what happened next, but she heard Ariadne say, "Like this?" There was a pause, and then she heard Karl say very softly, *"Exactly* like that . . ."

He rested his hands on Emma's shoulders and pushed himself up straight again. He stood behind her, close to the camera. There was silence all along the canal. Ariadne, her eyes closed, gave a little smile.

"I am ready, Karl," she said.

Karl nodded to Bob to switch on the camera.

"OK, Ariadne," said Karl quietly. "Open your eyes, look straight at the camera, and think about—Leonidas . . ."

Ariadne opened her eyes. Her look hit Emma like an electric shock. She felt a sudden dizzying sense of ecstasy, and all the fine hairs along her arms stood on end.

"Good girl," murmured Karl.

He raised his voice to its normal level.

"OK, boys, cut and print it."

In silence the double boat returned to the landing-stage. Emma glanced at the camera crew as they stumbled out on to the steps, looking like men lost in a dream. They too had felt the shock of Ariadne thinking about Leonidas.

Surely, thought Emma, no unknown ever had such a bunch of godfathers—Karl Meister to direct her, František to light her, Brock Berowne and Richard Traherne to be her leading men. She thought sadly of the actors and actresses she knew, making the depressing and humiliating round of agents and auditions, waiting for phone calls that didn't come.

Beth, Babs and Charles Make-Up fussed around Ariadne, showered her with congratulations, and led her in triumph up the great staircase to where an anxious Leonidas awaited her in her dressing-room—the star dressing-room that had once been Stella Camay's.

Stephen had been right.

"The Queen is dead. Long live the Queen!"

A few nights later, a small group walked into a scruffy little cinema near the Palazzo Pavone. The last of the audience was drifting out, and the projectionist was lacing up the print of Ariadne's tests. Karl and Walther sat near the back of the cinema, with the crew ranged around them: František and the camera crew, Gerry and the sound crew, Hal, Marco and Emma. They were tense and very quiet. The atmosphere was hot and stuffy, stale with the cigarette smoke and sweat of the departed audience. As Walther lit up a cheroot, Frank Jones the Production Manager came down from the projection box.

"Ready when you are, Karl," he said.

"Roll 'em," said Karl.

The cinema darkened and the white beam of the projector cut through the blue haze. Numbers flashed on the screen— 10, 9, 8, 7, 6, 5, 4, 3—then there was a confused jumble of heads bobbing about in front of the camera, then the clapperboard and a voice calling, "Testing Ariadne Andros." The clapperboard shut with a crack like a whip.

Ariadne and Richard Traherne appeared on the screen, and for once nobody looked at Richard. Ariadne was enchanting.

She's no actress, thought Emma, but you can't take your eyes off her.

Finally they came to the big close-up. This was the make-or-break shot. Emma held her breath, and sensed that everybody else was doing the same. Ariadne's exquisite face, eyes closed, filled the screen. Her eyelids fluttered open. Her face seemed to light up from within, and a faint blush crept up her throat. Her lips parted, and her big dark eyes looked straight at the audience. A quiver ran through the darkened cinema, and Emma heard a faint sigh from someone sitting near her. Star quality . . .

"Good girl," murmured Karl. "Good girl, Ariadne . . ."

The picture ran out in a series of bright flashes and scratches, and the screen blazed white. The projector was switched off, and the audience sat in darkness until the house lights slowly came up. For a long time nobody spoke. The only sound came from the projection box, where the projectionist was hastily wrapping up for the night.

At last Karl said, carefully casual, "Well, I guess she'll do," and walked with Walther towards the exit. As they reached the door he paused and turned, his arm on Walther's shoulder.

"No publicity!" he said. "We'll keep Ariadne under wraps until we get back to the States. Those tests are OK, but we've a long way to go yet, and we may still end up with egg on our faces. Where's *der* Wop?"

Marco made a slight movement, and Karl turned towards him.

"Marco! Tell Ariadne she's going to replace Stella, but don't make a fuss of her. She's got a lot to learn, and I don't want her turning into a spoiled brat. Frank, you get out a contract for her first thing in the morning. OK, Walther?"

"Aber ja, Herr Kapitän," said Walther. And he laughed.

" 'Night, boys," said Karl. He turned and went out with Walther. The door closed behind them.

The unit was fizzing with excitement.

If you are in the film business, then nothing, *nothing,* compares with the thrill of watching a new star appear on the screen for the first time. Columbus discovering America? Newton discovering gravity? Peanuts.

Chattering like starlings at twilight, they tumbled out of the cinema and made for the nearest bar.

Later that night, as Emma walked back to her hotel, she wondered idly if Ariadne had any idea of the glittering future that lay before her. Then, not so idly, she wondered what kind of contract Karl would offer her. He had found a star, and he

knew it. Ariadne would zoom skywards, and anyone attached
to her with a nice strong contract would zoom with her.

There was, of course, one contract supposed to be even
stronger than a business one, and that was the marriage contract. Leonidas would find himself soaring up with Ariadne.
How would he like it? Would he be proud of his wife, or
jealous of her success?

Emma shook herself impatiently. It was none of her business.

The news that Ariadne was to replace Stella reached Stephen
early the next morning, and the implications suddenly dawned
on him. He hurried to confide them to Emma.

"B-but it will m-mean re-shooting all Stella's scenes!" he
cried. "All those gondolas on the c-canal, and the m-masked
revels, and the abduction! And we're supposed to be g-going
to La Rocca—"

"Calm down!" said Emma. "Give Karl the credit for knowing at least as much about his shooting schedule as you do!"

Stephen reddened awkwardly.

"Didn't you notice," said Emma, "that what were supposed
to be 'tests' of Ariadne were in fact re-takes of all Stella's close
shots?"

"C-close shots, yes," said Stephen. "B-but what about all
the other scenes where Stella was seen with other p-people?"

"Stella was wearing a head-dress that covered her blond
hair," said Emma, "and a lot of the time she had her mask over
her face. You remember that Ariadne wore the same costume
for her tests, and we couldn't see her hair."

"You m-mean," said Stephen, "that b-because the audience
will see Ariadne in the c-close shots, they will assume that it's
Ariadne b-behind the mask in the long shots?"

"That's right," said Emma.

Stephen moved away, then swung back, his comical owlet
face mournful.

"It will be as if Stella had n-never existed, w-won't it?" he said.

"Yes," said Emma. "As if Stella had never existed."

"Poor Stella," said Stephen.

Emma thought of the black gondola gliding over the dark waters of the canal, the look on the face of the gondolier, the white figure of Stella lying in the boat, and the rest of that terrible night.

"Poor Stella," she said.

Later that night, as she lay in bed, Emma thought about Stella Camay's death. Hal was right, you couldn't have everybody suspecting everybody else of murder. But all the same . . .

She thought about the magazine story of possible wartime betrayal. She thought about the mixed nationalities of the unit. The Meisters were naturalized Americans, formerly German; František was naturalized British, formerly Czech; Leonidas was Greek; she supposed that all the rest of the unit were either English or Italian. But they were all people who had lived their very different lives before they came together by chance to make this one film. Any one of them might have reason to avenge an act of treachery ten years earlier.

She thought about Karl. If Stella had betrayed somebody close to him, then Karl might very well have murdered her.

Walther? She smiled to herself. He'd make a hash of it. Probably murder the wrong person.

Drowsily she reviewed the whole unit and considered practically every one as a possible murderer. She even thought about Stephen. She didn't want to suspect him. She *liked* Stephen. But just for a moment she wondered. Could he really be as ingenuous as he seemed? Could anybody so interested in films know so little about film-making? Could he have engineered that invitation from Karl for some sinister purpose? Sinister? *Stephen?* She laughed at the very idea, and drifted off to sleep.

Almost at once she jerked wide awake. She thought of Brock Berowne, who had arrived so unexpectedly one evening in the Piazza San Marco. Brock's explanation of his arrival had been so feeble that she had accepted it without question—such things do happen. But—could he have had some other reason for arriving so early at the location? And there was something else that she remembered—Brock reading the off-screen line "Not so fast, my lady!" that made Stella scream so very convincingly. Was that merely the response of an actress to a first-class actor, or was it possible that Brock had seized the opportunity to whisper a line that conveyed a real menace to Stella?

And yet she could not imagine Brock poisoning anyone. She could imagine him smothering Stella, and quoting Othello as he did so. But poison? No.

By the time Emma fell asleep she had been through the entire unit list, and the only person she did not consider for a moment as a possible murderer was Hal.

8

Commissario Gabrieli frowned as he gazed unseeing out of his office window at the canal. Sunbeams danced on the water, and small spangles of reflected light quivered on the wall opposite, but he was not aware of them. The click of the telephone being replaced made him turn and look across the room.

"The film unit," said Calvi. "They're leaving Venice tomorrow. We can't stop them, can we?"

The Commissario shook his head.

"Where are they going?" he said.

"They'll be filming at a place called La Rocca," said Calvi.

"There are hundreds of places called La Rocca," said Gabrieli. "Which one is it?"

"Somewhere near Lucca," said Calvi. "That's where their production office will be. I have their phone number."

The slowly revolving electric fan stirred a few papers on his desk. He shifted his elbow to pin them down more securely.

"You know," he said, "I can see that it would have been possible to poison Karl Meister's food—*his* lunch-box was set apart from all the others. Somebody could have replaced it with a similar box containing poisoned food and nobody would have noticed the substitution. But it was *Stella Camay* who died—and there was no way of knowing which box would be delivered to her."

"According to Signor Marco," said Gabrieli, "he picked up three apparently identical boxes—one from the ledge and two from the table. Plenty of people saw him do it. He put one box on Karl Meister's desk, one on Mr. Walther's desk, and one on

Stella Camay's dressing-table. *But he doesn't know which box he gave to Stella Camay."*

Calvi looked at him.

"Poison in the box on the ledge?" he said. "In the ordinary way it would have been given to Karl Meister. But this was not an ordinary day. Signor Marco picked up two more boxes from the table—and I think they must have been harmless. Do you think he delivered the harmless ones to Karl Meister and his cousin, and the poisoned one to Stella Camay?"

"I think it's a possibility," said Gabrieli.

"Somebody after Karl Meister?"

"Yes."

"They didn't succeed."

"No," said Gabrieli. "But they might try again . . ."

Nobody in the film unit was sorry to leave Venice, despite the sunshine flashing and sparkling on the lagoon. The dark memory of Stella Camay's death hung over the place, and everyone was glad to be going. They could hardly have found a better contrast. Where Venice floated upon the water like an elegant nest of swans, La Rocca perched like an eagle's eyrie on a bare, rocky hill which rose like a sugar-loaf from the plain below. The convoy of cars and trucks ground its way slowly up the narrow, bumpy road which snaked up the hill to a dry, dusty little square with a bar, some petrol pumps, a few shuttered shops, a few empty benches under the dusty plane-trees, and a few cats dozing in the sunshine. From the square a steep, stony track climbed to the top of the hill. And there for the first time they saw the castle which gave the place its name: La Rocca. The castle itself was nothing but a few ruined walls, but the Art Department had transformed it into a stern grey fortress with crenellated walls and, high above them, the black and silver standard of Prince Leone Volpe, better known as Brock Berowne.

The standard drooped in the stillness of the mid-day heat, and Karl pointed this out. The Art Director shouted at some unseen subordinate, and the standard suddenly opened as though it had been jerked by a string. Another shout, and the standard fluttered proudly. Then the string broke, and the standard drooped again. Karl pointed this out, too, and then went off with Walther to have a closer look at the castle gates.

The rest of the unit climbed out of their vehicles, stretching themselves after the long drive from Venice. They hoped Karl wasn't going to stay long—they hadn't had lunch yet. They probably wouldn't get any until they reached Lucca, and how far away was that? Stephen looked at the castle and wondered what the rooms inside would be like. A baronial hall, perhaps, hung with flags and flaring torches, a high, smoke-blackened timber roof, and a floor covered with rushes.

"D-do you think I could g-go inside the castle when K-Karl's finished looking at the g-gates?" he asked.

"Oh, don't wait for Karl," said Emma. "He'll be ages yet. Go round the side."

Stephen set off to look for a side entrance.

He knew that the front wall of the castle was a fake, the work of the Art Department. It had not occurred to him that there would be no side walls at all. But behind the façade lay nothing but a great open space, bigger than the entire town of La Rocca. At the far end was another high wall, apparently the twin of the castle entrance but lacking the massive gateway. Both walls were built up on a scaffolding of tubular steel struts, and high up, behind the battlements, were walkways of wooden planks.

Over to his left, well away from the castle, stood a large barn, and beyond it a smaller building. Stephen hoped it contained latrines. He suddenly appreciated the lost luxury of working conditions at the Palazzo Pavone.

He turned back to survey the castle's open-air interior again. Chunks of unfinished scenery were scattered about. A cluster of stone walls made of painted canvas leaned together, propped uncertainly against some oil-drums. As Stephen watched, one of the drums rolled away, making a hollow sound as it bumped over the stony ground, and the walls collapsed. At his feet lay rows of tubular struts and clamps, looking like pieces of a giant Meccano set. Beside them stood a spiral staircase which would have looked quite at home in the Tower of London, but here was free-standing, corkscrewing its way up towards the sky and showing its rough wooden interior and plaster-covered steps.

Men were busy carrying ladders, carrying buckets, building platforms, hammering, sweating, each one intent upon his job. Raucous music was blaring from a radio somewhere in the distance, and Stephen was unaccountably reminded of his childhood, when he used to watch the fairground showmen setting up the Bank Holiday fair on the Common. They had bustled about just like these men, putting up the Helter-Skelter—not unlike the spiral staircase—and the Haunted House —the hollow-sounding drum and the collapsing stone walls might do for that—and the Wall of Death, where motorbikes screamed and zoomed and thrilled the crowds. The rear wall of the castle would serve for the Wall of Death. But where were the galloping horses of the roundabout, the dodgem cars and the Giant Switchback? Where was the blissful scent of bruised grass, and the distant smell of fried onions?

Stephen smiled to himself. Living on a film unit with Karl and Walther Meister, who needed dodgem cars and Giant Switchbacks? And it was ridiculous to try to conjure up the scent of grass in this high, bare place, while as for fried on-ions—! He sniffed. He sniffed again. He *could* smell fried on-ions.

He suddenly realized that he was hungry.

Somebody came out of the barn and banged a gong.

Food!

The construction men stopped work and headed for the barn. Stephen followed them, and found the rest of the film unit streaming in the same direction. He saw Marco ahead, and hurried to catch up with him.

"I say, M-Marco," he said, "what's that wooden building over there? Is it a toilet?"

"No," said Marco. "The toilets are on the other side. That building is a stable."

"A stable!" breathed Stephen. "Are we g-going to have horses here?"

"Oh yes," said Marco. "There will be about twenty, I suppose."

Galloping horses—not the painted wooden horses of a fairground roundabout, but the real thing. Stephen sighed happily and followed Marco into the barn.

It was an open-sided building, with translucent walls made of light straw matting which could be rolled up or down as required. At the moment the matting hung down like a curtain, cutting out the glare of the sun. Inside, the barn was laid out as a cafeteria, with a service area near the kitchens at one end, and long rows of trestle tables down each side. There was a general hubbub of conversation, and a continuous blare of music from a transistor radio in the kitchen. Marco and Stephen joined the queue at the serving counter, and looked around them.

Karl and Walther sat at a long table with the Art Director. Emma, Hal and Dave the stunt man joined them. Frank Jones the Production Manager collected his tray, and at a signal from Karl went over and sat beside him.

"Hey, Marco, come and join us," said Karl. "We're having a production meeting."

Marco put his tray on the table and sat down. As there was an empty seat beside him, Stephen sat down also. He looked at the enormous bowl of steaming pasta and wondered if he would be able to eat it all. He was hungry, yes, but . . .

"As of now we're going to be based at Lucca," said Karl. "We shall be shooting here at La Rocca for about six weeks. Then in late June we do some shots in the countryside round about. On July 2nd we go to Siena to film the Palio horse-race.

My wife saw it a few years back, and she was crazy about it. Now, Marco, tell us about the Palio."

"The Palio is a very old institution," said Marco. "It has a charter dating back to—1310, I think—"

"Spare us the history," said Karl. "Just give us the goddam facts."

"The Palio is a horse-race which is run in the main square of Siena," said Marco. "Before the race there is a big parade in mediaeval costume—very much like the costumes in our film."

"You all know the story outline," said Karl. "We'll fill it in later, but basically at the climax of the film we have Richard riding in the Palio—he wins of course—and afterwards he and Brock have a fight to the death—Richard wins, of course, and he and Ariadne ride off into the sunset. End titles. I want plenty of action and plenty of production value. Now, Marco, has the Palio got action and production value?"

Emma thought she saw a momentary gleam of anger in Marco's eyes, but he answered courteously.

"The Palio takes place in the main square of Siena—the Campo—it is very old and very beautiful. Everybody wears mediaeval costume. The race itself is always full of incident. The jockeys ride without saddles, they try to unhorse each other, and very often they succeed. The Palio is a form of jousting, and it is for real."

"How many horses do they have?" asked Karl.

"Ten," said Marco.

"Frank, have Wardrobe make up ten costumes matching the ones used by the jockeys—Richard will wear the costume of the rider who actually wins the race on July 2nd. We'll use long shots of the actual race, and cut in closer shots of Richard. We'll get away with that—plus plenty of shots of the fancy costumes."

"The spectators are of course in modern dress," said Marco. "One hundred thousand people watch the race, and ten thousand of them are standing in the centre of the Campo."

"We'll keep the camera off them," said Karl. "Where can we stage the big fight between Brock and Richard? I want somewhere with a great flight of steps so that Brock can really take a tumble—I want him to die head down, with that big cloak of his spilling down the steps like a black waterfall."

"Brock could never fight in that cloak!" said Emma. "It weighs a ton."

"He can throw it off at the start of the fight, and Richard can drape it over him when he's dead," snapped Karl. "Now, Luciano, can you give me a flight of steps where Brock and Richard can fight it out?"

"Sure thing, dottore," said Luciano.

"In Siena?"

"Sure," said Luciano. "The Duomo—the cathedral—that has a fine staircase and plenty of production value. No sweat."

"Right," said Karl. "Tomorrow we go to Siena, have a look at the Campo and the cathedral. Meet me in the Campo at midday."

"Excuse me, Mr. Meister," said Marco. "I suggest we all meet by the bell-tower—the Campo is a big place."

"Right," said Karl. "Bell-tower, Campo, midday tomorrow. OK, Walther?"

"Aber ja, Herr Kapitän," said Walther. And he laughed.

As soon as lunch was ended, Frank Jones and Hal shepherded the unit back into the cars and led the way to Lucca. Stephen slept most of the way—he had managed to eat all the pasta, and a good deal more besides—and awoke to find himself driving through a massive archway into a walled city.

"We'd better take the crew round to their different hotels," said Frank Jones. "If we leave them to find their own way they'll get lost."

Stephen had a confused picture of small streets and very large churches, and amphitheatre like an empty bull-ring, and everywhere towers, towers, towers. One very ancient tower even had trees growing out of the top. At various hotels scattered about the city they dropped members of the crew, and at last entered the hotel which was going to serve as headquarters for the duration of the film.

"Where's Richard staying?" asked Hal.

"He's rented a converted farmhouse," said Frank. "He and his wife and Yorky will be self-contained as usual."

"Ariadne and Leonidas?"

"They're in a nice little hotel round the corner from here," said Frank. "I've put Marco there too, since he's a friend of theirs—and he'll make sure they turn up on time for their calls. They can travel with him to and from work."

"Where's Karl staying?" asked Emma.

"He and Walther have fixed to stay at a villa a few miles out in the country—guests of some American contessa," said Frank. "The estate has woods and fields and olive groves, and when Karl talks about filming in the countryside, that's the countryside he's thinking of. I hope the contessa knows what she's in for . . ."

The Reception Clerk completed the registration formalities and handed out their keys.

"Signorina Shah-va, Signor Ellivella, Signor Franco Yoness and Signor Lo-vay-lah-chay," he said.

Emma Shaw, Hal Halliwell and Frank Jones recognized themselves and claimed their keys. Stephen did not.

"Come on, Stephen," said Frank Jones. "You may be Mr. Lovelace in England, but over here you're Signor Lo-vay-lah-chay. You might as well get used to it."

Later that afternoon, having unpacked and taken a shower, Emma set out to explore Lucca. She looked at the Teatro del Giglio, did some window-shopping, admired the municipal flowerbeds, and found herself at the foot of the city wall. Traffic was getting busy, and to get away from it she climbed a slope which would, she thought, bring her to the top of the wall where there might be some fresh air, and a view of the

city. Expecting to find only a narrow walkway, she was astonished to find herself in a broad tree-lined avenue thirty feet
above the street. There was a little breeze, for which she was
grateful. She sat down on a bench and prepared to watch the
people of Lucca strolling under the trees. A familiar figure
came along, head down, studying a tourist map.

"Ciao, Stephen!" she said.

"Emma!"

Stephen hurried towards her.

"Isn't this wonderful?"

He sat down beside her.

"Isn't this a fantastic little place?" he said. "It's L-Lilliput!
I've walked all round it along these w-walls, and I d-don't
suppose I've done five m-miles! Is Siena anything like this?"

"It's an old walled city like this," said Emma, "but it's very
much bigger. I went there once—it was just an overnight stop.
There's a cathedral like a stack of liquorice allsorts—the black
and white striped ones—and it's got a striped tower too."

"What's the square like, where they run the P-Palio?"

"Oh, that's beautiful," said Emma. "It's like a great scallop
shell. And there's a lovely bell-tower simply rocketing up into
the sky—they say it's the most beautiful bell-tower in the
world. I remember I sat in the Campo in the evening, and
watched the full moon hanging over the tower, and I thought
to myself, 'You can keep the Taj Mahal—*I've* seen the Torre
Mangia by moonlight.' "

They sat quietly side by side, lost in their thoughts, until the
breeze tugged at the map in Stephen's hands, and he began to
fold it up.

"I got this m-map because I'm going to have a look round
and see if I can f-find somewhere cheaper to stay," he said.
"I'll have a couple of d-days living in the l-lap of luxury, but
after that I shall have to move out."

"It's a shame that you have to pay for your hotel out of your own pocket," said Emma. "If ever you get stuck, I'm sure some of us would help—"

"N-no, really, Emma, it's all right," said Stephen hurriedly. "Thanks all the same, but really I'm m-managing better than I anticipated. You see, I'd expected to have to pay my own t-travelling expenses when the unit moved, but I came here in the c-car with you and Hal for free. And I'd expected to pay for my food, but eating with the unit means I've hardly had to spend anything at all on that. The lunch-boxes have absolutely saved my l-life—"

He broke off, thinking unhappily of one particular lunch-box that had been the means of death.

"Emma," he said awkwardly, "I've been thinking about Stella Camay, and I d-don't think that lunch-box was intended for her at all. I think it was intended for K-Karl. The wrong person was k-killed."

"But why should anybody want to murder Karl?" said Emma. "Oh, I know we all say we feel like it now and again, even Hacker says he feels like it, and I say it myself at least once a day—but not *seriously.*"

"If K-Karl died, what would happen to the film?" asked Stephen.

"Somebody else would take over," said Emma.

"Hal?" asked Stephen.

"No, the management would send some big director from Hollywood to take it over."

"What about Walther?" asked Stephen.

"Walther!" said Emma. "Oh no, the management would never let Walther do it!"

"Do you think," said Stephen diffidently, "d-do you think Walther realizes that?"

Emma looked at him for a moment.

"Walther *might* see himself as the great director," she said slowly. "Nobody else would, but *he* might."

She remembered how she had considered Walther as a possible murderer, and had rejected the idea with some amuse-

ment on the grounds that Walther would probably have murdered the wrong person. If Stephen was right, and the
intended victim was not Stella Camay but Karl Meister, then
the wrong person had been murdered. But Walther—no, she
could not believe it.

"Hal's right, Stephen," she said. "We mustn't play at being
detectives. We shall only end up by suspecting each other, and
I for one couldn't do my job properly if I thought the person
beside me was a murderer. Come on, let's take a walk along
the walls and have a look at Lilliput . . ."

9

Next morning those members of the crew involved in the reconnaissance arrived in Siena well before midday so that they could have a look at the place before their rendezvous with Karl at the bell-tower in the Campo. L. J. Hacker was anxious to see the setting for the final scenes that he was going to have to write, and he hitched a lift for himself and Winifred in the car of Art Director Luciano. On arrival in Siena, Luciano muttered that he had to see somebody about something and, pointing vaguely in the direction of the Campo, left the Hackers to find their own way there. Ten minutes later they were hopelessly lost, picking their way up and down a maze of steep cobbled streets. Then Hacker caught sight of Hal striding along, head and shoulders above everybody else. The Hackers tagged on to Hal's party, which consisted of František, the camera crew, Emma, Marco and Stephen.

Stephen had no idea where he was going. He kept following Marco and Emma, his eyes darting to left and right as he tried to take in everything at once. Suddenly Marco swung off to his left down a short, steep street. The rest of the unit carried on window-shopping, but Emma and Stephen followed Marco and found themselves on the edge of the Campo.

Instinctively they stopped dead and stared at the great open space, so calm after the bustle of the grey canyons they had just come through.

"B-but it's—enormous!" said Stephen at last. "It's like finding yourself alone on the pitch at Wembley Stadium! It's j-just —well—it's just *space*. And quiet. Right in the m-middle of the city!"

Marco smiled.

"To me," he said, "it is as though one steps from a noisy market-place into the peace of a great cathedral."

"Let's find somewhere to sit and just look at it," said Emma. They passed a chemist's shop called Farmacia Mossa.

"See, Stephen," said Marco. "*Farmacia* means 'a pharmacy' —a drugstore. And *Mossa* means 'the start of a race.' The Palio starts outside that shop."

Next to the pharmacy was a café with the chairs and tables set out on the pavement. In contrast to the garish colours of the other cafés in the Campo, this one had chairs and table-cloths of dark blue. They sat down, gave their orders to a waiter, and looked at the Campo.

"You were right, Emma," said Stephen. "It really is like a b-big scallop shell."

Around the great expanse of the Campo curved a solid wall of high houses, terracotta, grey and ochre, some topped with square crenellations and pierced with gothic arched windows, others with tall windows flanked by shutters and provided with narrow balconies. All were roofed with crinkly red tiles. The ground floors of most of the houses were given over to small souvenir shops and cafés with bright chairs, tables and sun-shades. A number of dark streets cut their way between the shops and the Campo, like very small spokes fitted to a very large hub.

"I s-say, Marco," said Stephen, "what's that b-building down there on the right?"

"That is the Palazzo Pubblico," said Marco. "You would say —the Town Hall, isn't it?"

"And—oh, look," murmured Emma. "There's the Torre Mangia . . ."

"The Torre Mangia," echoed Marco softly. "The most beautiful bell-tower in the world . . ."

The slender tower of rose-red brick soaring up from the side of the Palazzo Pubblico was topped with a white corolla of buttressed parapets. Above it sprang the bell-chamber itself, dazzling white against the brilliant blue sky. And suspended above the whiteness, a great bronze bell.

They sat and stared at it.

"Just look at all those p-pigeons," said Stephen. "It's just like the P-Piazza San Marco, or T-Trafalgar Square. C-croo-croo . . . croo-croo . . ."

Groups of pigeons waddled in purposeful formation over the Campo, a solid phalanx of bright pink feet and dark grey wings echoing the colours of the pavement underneath them. As Emma and Stephen watched idly, all the bells of Siena began to ring for noon, and the pigeons rose in a single movement, sweeping up and away, the pale grey of their breasts and bellies changing into the dark grey of their backs as they wheeled over with the precision of an aerobatic squadron. Up and up they flew until they circled the pale coronet of the Torre Mangia, where the great bell Sunto was booming out the twelve strokes.

"Marco, have you ever seen the Palio?" asked Emma.

"Only once," said Marco slowly. "It was—wonderful. For a long time afterwards I was filled with a great desire to make a film of it—not as a spectacular piece of production value, as Mr. Meister will do, but—I think you would say—as an act of homage to something beautiful and very, very old. I do not belong to Siena, but when I watch the Palio again this year—oh, how I shall wish that I did!"

Hal and his party had arrived and were sitting outside a café opposite the Palazzo Pubblico. The Hackers were clearly feeling the heat, and Emma noticed that Winifred had eased her feet out of her shoes.

"Oh, l-look!" said Stephen. "I think this is going to be f-funny!"

Karl and Walther, followed at a slight distance by the stunt men Dave and Johnny, were making their way across the Campo towards the café where Hal's party was sitting. There was a sudden flurry of activity. Bills were called for and paid at great speed, and by the time Karl and Walther arrived, only Mr. and Mrs. Hacker remained, although they too were in the process of settling their bill.

"Hi, Hack!" called Karl, and the Hackers rose furiously to their feet. Mrs. Hacker then sat down again suddenly because one foot had not gone back into its shoe, and Hacker knelt down and helped her to get it on.

"Excuse us for a minute, Karl," he said. "We just want to buy a street-map before the shops close for lunch. See you at the bell-tower . . ."

"See you in church," said Walther. And he laughed.

Emma was glad to see Dave and Johnny sitting near Karl. Ever since Stephen's suggestion that the poisoned lunch-box had been intended for Karl, she had been feeling uneasy about him. But nobody was likely to try to poison him at the café, and if he needed a bodyguard he could hardly have anything better than his two leading stunt men.

"Let's go to the bell-tower," she said. "The rendezvous was supposed to be midday, and it's past that already."

They walked down the slope of the Campo, distancing themselves discreetly from Karl and Walther.

"We're the first to arrive, anyway," said Emma, turning to look at the big wooden doors set into the wall of the Palazzo Pubblico.

"What enormous d-doors!" said Stephen. "Where do they l-lead?"

"Into a courtyard, I think," said Marco.

"I like the little d-door at the side," said Stephen. "It looks a b-bit like a cat-flap."

"Shall we go through?" said Marco. "I do not suppose that Mr. Meister and Mr. Walther will come until everybody has got here."

He led the way through the cat-flap, and they found themselves in a cool courtyard set with a forest of brick pillars rising to a vaulted roof, the middle part of it open to the sky. They looked up through the opening, and by craning their heads far back, could see all the way up to the top of the bell-tower soaring dizzily above them, leaning towards them and seemingly ready to crash down over them like a gigantic tidal wave.

"It makes me feel giddy," said Emma, and to restore her balance she looked down at the floor with its herring-bone bricks. Then she turned and looked out through the cat-flap towards the Campo. To the right of the big double doors was a high window, unglazed, but protected by a wrought iron grille. She could see a clover-leaf shape worked into the plain squares of the grille, and then, as her eyes became accustomed to the gloom of the courtyard, she saw a small dark door, heavily barred and very narrow, marked *"Ingresso alla Torre."*

"That is the way up to the top of the tower," said Marco. "It is quite a climb. Three hundred and thirty-two steps . . ."

Stephen was looking at a notice by the door. *"Chiuso."*

"Key-uso," he said. "Does that mean it's closed?"

"That is right," said Marco. "Your knowledge of Italian is improving."

"Yes," said Stephen. "I have quite a vocabulary. 'Key-uso' means that it's closed, and 'non chay' means that whatever I want is not available. Very helpful . . ."

"You know *prego* and *grazie* too," said Marco. "I've heard you."

"And I hope you know the names on the public toilets," said Emma with a smile.

"Well," said Stephen, "m-most of them seem to be m-marked 'Uomini,' and that obviously means 'women,' so I d-don't go in them. I d-don't know the word for 'men.' I wish I did."

Marco and Emma laughed.

"Stephen, *uomini* means 'men.' It's the plural of *uomo,* meaning 'a man,' " said Emma.

"As in *Homo sapiens,* you know," said Marco helpfully. " 'Intelligent man.' "

"I m-must be the original un-intelligent m-man," said Stephen. "I wish I'd known that b-before."

"Here comes Hal," said Emma, and led the way out into the sunshine again.

Hal arrived with František and the camera crew. Hacker followed, clutching his script.

"Winifred decided to stay and have an ice," he said to Hal. "She's a little shy—doesn't want to intrude while we're working."

Emma glanced across the Campo to where Winifred Hacker was sitting at a table under a large sunshade advertising Campari. Mrs. Hacker didn't look particularly shy. She just looked as though she had done quite enough walking for one day.

"It's quite a size, this Campo," said Bob, the camera operator. "But how the devil do they run a horse-race here, Marco? You're not going to tell me the horses race over this pavement —if they fell, they'd break their legs!"

"No, no," said Marco. "The horses do not run on the pavement. There is a race-track made of earth which is put down round the outer edge of the Campo—it is a little like a doughnut ring—and the horses run round and round the Campo on the track."

"How do you watch it, then?" asked Bob.

"If you are a very important person," said Marco, "you watch it from the stands of the Palazzo Pubblico. Otherwise you watch from the stands that are set up in front of the shops —if you can afford the price of a ticket. And if you cannot afford it, then you stand in a great crowd in the middle. They say that one hundred thousand people watch the race, and ten thousand of them stand in the crowd in the middle. Of course the people in the crowd do not see so much as the people in the stands, but if you are not important or rich you have to take what you can get."

Karl and Walther arrived. Dave and Johnny followed, and perched themselves on a couple of stone bollards.

"Right, Marco," said Karl, "give us a run-down on the Palio."

Marco stood with his back to the bell-tower and looked across the Campo. The others followed his gaze.

"If we think of the Campo as a clock," said Marco, "then here at the bell-tower we are standing at about six o'clock. The Fonte Gaia—that blue water facing us at the top of the slope—that is twelve o'clock. The parade begins at that street up there on the left—call it ten o'clock—then it goes all round the Campo and ends in front of the Palazzo Pubblico—over there on our left—somewhere between seven and eight o'clock. The race for the Palio begins outside that café up there on the left —the one with the dark blue tables and chairs. It follows the same course as the parade, but the horses have to make three complete circuits of the Campo."

"That corner over there on our right—what's it called?" said Karl.

"The Martino corner," said Marco.

"The pavement runs down hill there, and it's right on the bend. Is that where most of the spills happen?" asked Karl.

"Yes," said Marco. "The Martino is a very dangerous corner."

"We better plan on having a camera somewhere about here, then," said Karl. "Facing the bell-tower, able to pan from the Martino corner to the end of the race."

"Where's that?" asked Walther.

"Just past the Palazzo Pubblico," said Marco.

"Right," said Karl. "Four cameras in the centre of the Campo—one for the start, one for the middle where the blue water is—one at the bell-tower, and one at the finish. Now let's go look at the Cathedral. Which way, Hack?"

Hacker looked flustered.

"Thought you were going to buy a street-map, Hack," said Karl, with a crocodile grin. "Never mind, never mind, scrub the street-map, Marco can take us to the Cathedral."

He nodded to Marco, and started off at a fast pace, his arm

round Walther's shoulder. The others followed. Hacker hurried across the Campo, collected his wife and hustled her as fast as he could after the departing crew. He had no wish to be lost in Siena again. As they hurried along he wondered uneasily how they were going to get back to Lucca. He hoped the Art Director was still around. A few minutes later they reached the front of the Cathedral, and to Hacker's delight, Luciano was waiting for them there. The problem of transport for the return to Lucca was solved.

Luciano bounded up to Karl.

"Here it is, *dottore,*" he said. "The Duomo of Siena! How is that for production value?"

The Duomo of Siena is one of the most spectacular pieces of gothic architecture ever raised to the glory of God.

It is big.

It is striped like a football jersey in broad bands of black and white.

It has three huge doors, flanked by twisted stone columns like giant sticks of barley sugar. Above them is a rose window of the Last Supper, and paintings showing the Glorification of the Virgin Mary.

There are spires and turrets, and turrets upon turrets.

There are winged horses and lions leaping into space, and what appears to be the entire cast of the Old Testament carved in stone.

It is production value par excellence.

Karl Meister glared at it.

"Too goddam fussy!" he said. "I need a *plain* background for the fight. Against all that razzamatazz the audience won't even notice Brock and Richard."

"But, *dottore,* production value," said Luciano. "You said you wanted production value!"

"Forget it," said Karl. "Scrub the Duomo. Right, Walther?"

"*Aber ja, Herr Kapitän,*" said Walther. And he laughed.

Luciano looked ready to burst into tears.

"Scrub the Duomo?" he said incredulously. His voice rose to a squeak. "Scrub the *Duomo?*"

"I told you before," said Karl. "I need a *plain* background for the fight. And I need a *steep* staircase so that Brock's cloak can spill down it."

He turned to Marco.

"Back to the car park," he said.

The crew's excitement vanished. They stood about, deflated and depressed, watching Marco as he led Karl and Walther, with Dave and Johnny close behind, along the side of the Cathedral. At the far end Marco took Karl down a steep flight of steps.

At the foot of the steps Marco paused for a moment and looked back as though waiting for the rest of the crew to catch up. Karl took a few paces forward, realized that he didn't know how to find the car park, and turned back angrily.

"Come on, Marco, come on!" he snapped. "We haven't got—"

And then he saw the steps that he had just walked down.

Broad stone steps leading up to the side of the Duomo, its bands of black and white marble plain and uncluttered. At the top of the steps, a doorway.

"Dave! Johnny!" shouted Karl. "Go back up there and do Brock's death fight on the steps!"

Dave and Johnny turned and ran up the steps towards the door at the top.

"Starting here, Karl?" called Dave.

"Make an entrance through the door!" shouted Karl. "Fight across and across, then back Richard down the steps, twist, and have him kill Brock somewhere in the middle there!"

By now Hal and the rest of the party had reached the top of the stairs, but Hal pulled everybody back out of the way. They waited, and watched, as Dave and Johnny rehearsed the fight. At the end, Johnny ran Dave through with an imaginary sword. Dave staggered and fell dead.

"HAL!" roared Karl.

Hal appeared at the top of the steps.

"We do the fight here!" shouted Karl. "Come on down, all of you—not you, Dave. You and Johnny stay right there."

Hal and the others came down the steps, skirting round Dave, who had draped himself more comfortably along one of the steps, while the victorious Johnny stood guard over him. They gathered round Karl and looked up at the scene.

"We shoot the fight here," said Karl. "But why didn't the Art Department find this place instead of dragging me to that crazy three-ring circus? Why do I have to do all the work on this goddam picture? Why do I have to find my own locations?"

Emma wondered about that. Had Karl really discovered the steps on his own, or had Marco led him there?

"What's this place called, Marco?" asked Karl.

"Scala Sabatelli," said Marco. "The Sabatelli Steps."

Yes, it had been Marco's idea. Dear Marco. And he wouldn't get any credit for it. Karl was already quite sure that it was *his* discovery, and by the time they reached Lucca again it was a fair bet that Luciano would also be claiming it for his own.

"Hal, tell the Art Department we shoot the fight on the Sabatelli Steps," said Karl. "Come on, Dave, back to the car."

Everyone moved away, following Marco to the car park. The day had turned out well after all. Laughing and chattering, they piled into the cars and drove off.

The Hackers waited by the Art Director's car. When he did not show up, they retraced their steps to the front of the Duomo to look for him. He wasn't there.

When they returned to the car park, his car had gone.

Mr. and Mrs. Hacker returned to Lucca by a very slow bus.

10

The move to Lucca meant a change in the pattern of Emma's life. Meals on the location at La Rocca were taken at long tables in the noisy barn, so Hal, Marco and Stephen no longer gathered around her desk to share lunch-boxes and confidences. At Lucca itself she saw little of them. Stephen was staying in a small *pensione*. Marco was staying at a hotel with Leonidas and Ariadne, and spent his spare time with them. Sometimes when work was over for the day, Emma went out with Penny the Production Secretary to have dinner in a trattoria, but often they were both too tired to go out, so they ate alone in the empty hotel dining-room and then retired to their respective rooms. Emma often cried herself to sleep, for Hal was staying at the same hotel, and he might as well have been staying on the moon. She met him over breakfast coffee, she sat beside him as they travelled by car to and from La Rocca, but he was always preoccupied and silent. Perhaps it was the strain of working with Karl.

Karl drove the unit as hard as ever. Actors and technicians sweated through long hot days on the rocky hill-top. The stunt men had the worst of it, because they never had a rest. When they were not riding or fighting in front of the camera, they rehearsed riding and fighting with Leonidas, and at first that was even more exhausting. But Leonidas was learning. Emma noticed that Marco was devoting a lot of his time to Leonidas and Ariadne, and perhaps because of this, Ariadne became quietly professional, and the exuberant Leonidas began to perform his athletic feats within range of the camera. Walther, of course, took all the credit for anything that Leonidas or

Ariadne did, but apart from preening himself he did little but wander about the set, scribbling down ideas for scenes on the backs of envelopes. Emma simply could not imagine Walther as a murderer, and she put Stephen's suggestion out of her mind. The weeks rushed by, and Venice receded into a remote dream-world.

They completed shooting all the scenes at the front of the castle and moved to the rear wall. Stephen gave Emma a hand with her typewriter. They walked along a rough track that curved round to an area of stony waste ground. The Props men had already set up Emma's desk, and Stephen put the typewriter on it. Then he turned, and for the first time he looked up and saw the wall as it would appear to cinema audiences.

It was some forty feet high, topped with saw-toothed battlements. To the left and right, formidable grey stone towers jutted from the walls.

Stephen whistled.

"Wow!" he said. "The Wall of D-Death!"

Emma looked at him inquiringly.

"Oh," he said awkwardly, "the f-first time we came to La Rocca I w-watched the men b-building up bits of scenery, and I thought they were like showmen getting a f-fairground ready —and this w-wall reminded me of the Wall of D-Death."

"Not a bad name for it," said Emma. "This is where Richard and Leonidas come to rescue Ariadne—"

"Is she inside the c-castle, then?" asked Stephen. He had rather lost track of the story.

"Yes, Brock is keeping her prisoner here. Along come Richard and Leonidas to rescue her. Richard climbs over the wall —well, of course, Yorky does it really—but while he's doing that, Leonidas is killed by one of Brock's henchmen. So this really *is* a Wall of Death."

Stephen, impressed by the sheer scale of the walls when seen from below, trotted off to investigate them. A yard or two before he actually reached them he found his way barred by a thick hedge of small bushes, behind which he could see masses of cardboard cartons and old mattresses stacked along the whole length of the wall. Surprised and indignant, he trotted back to Emma.

"I s-say, Emma," he said, "somebody's dumped a whole lot of c-cartons behind those bushes—great b-big things, as b-big as armchairs!"

Emma took the news calmly.

"Can you see any of the boxes through the hedge?" she asked.

"N-no, I can't, but all the same—"

"That's all right, then," said Emma. "The hedge is there to screen the boxes, and the boxes are there for a very particular reason."

Stephen gaped at her.

"You mean—they're m-meant to be there?" he asked, simmering down slightly.

"That wall is as high as a house," said Emma. "Yorky has to climb up and over it, and if by any chance he should fall and land on the ground, he could be out of action for quite a while. But if he lands on a stack of big cardboard cartons, they will crumple under him and break his fall. And he can pick himself up and try again. You may have noticed that on this picture anything which is going to look dangerous on the screen is always very carefully rehearsed."

"I had n-noticed," said Stephen. He sounded a little disappointed.

"And there are always a number of safety precautions that one doesn't notice—like those fall-boxes. Let's face it—it's not just the stunt men—very often members of the crew can find themselves in dangerous situations. A good assistant director like Hal does his damnedest to look after us all—"

"I suppose Hal c-cares a lot about you p-people on the unit," said Stephen.

"I'm not sure that Hal cares about us as people," said Emma

thoughtfully. "I think he really only cares about the unit as a whole. If anybody gets hurt, then the whole unit is weakened, and we might even have to stop filming for a bit."

"You think it's more a c-case of 'the show must go on,' then?" said Stephen.

"I think that's more like it. But at any rate, if one is in a tight spot, then Hal's a good person to have around. If I had to climb that wall—and I hope I don't, because I've no head for heights—"

"Me neither," said Stephen.

"—but if I did have to climb that wall, and then, when I was up there, Hal told me to jump, I'd do it, because I'd know that he'd have organized some kind of safety net to break my fall."

"You must have a lot of faith in H-Hal," said Stephen. "I couldn't d-do it."

"Well, let's say I *think* I'd jump," said Emma. "By the way, are there any mattresses on top of the fall-boxes?"

"Yes," said Stephen. "Are they m-meant to be there too? I thought they were just d-dumped as rubbish."

"No, they help to break the fall. And the bushes were only planted yesterday—they're there to hide the boxes and the mattresses from the camera."

Stephen sighed.

"And I thought it was the other w-way round—I thought the b-bushes had been there a long t-time, and somebody was making use of them to d-dump their rubbish out of sight. This is a d-daft world!"

Richard and Yorky, wearing identical costumes, came on to the set with Leonidas, ready to rehearse. Yorky slipped away and disappeared behind a buttress against the wall of the left-hand tower.

"Is Yorky d-doubling for Richard in this scene?" asked Stephen.

"Yes—Richard is supposed to climb the wall, but in fact he'll duck behind that buttress over there—"

"B-but isn't that Yorky going behind the b-buttress now?"

"Yes. He'll wait out of sight, and then when Richard is hidden behind the buttress too, Yorky will appear and do the actual climb."

"And what's D-Dave doing?"

Dave, looking villainous in his black leather costume with heavy black gloves, was standing by a crossbow which stood a little way in back of the camera.

"Oh, he's playing the baddie who kills poor old Leo," said Emma.

Poor old Leo was looking very unhappy.

Richard went over to him.

"Cheer up, Leonidas," he said. "This is your big scene."

And he smiled.

"Big scene for me," said Leonidas. "I die—*endaxi*. Mr. Meister says many ladies in cinema will cry—*endaxi*. But *how* I die? I not understand."

"You die," said Richard cheerfully, "with a bolt between your shoulder-blades."

Leonidas looked even more unhappy.

Dave took off his black gloves and dropped them beside the crossbow. Then he came over, carrying a contraption of padding and wire, and a short black bolt with a square head. He showed the bolt to Leonidas.

"Looks nasty, doesn't it?" he said. "But you feel it, Leo. It's a trick bolt, made of balsa wood. Light as a feather, you know what I mean . . ."

Leonidas handled the bolt gingerly.

"This?" he said. "In my back? Will not *truly* kill me?"

"No, of course it won't truly kill you," said Dave. "Feel it."

Leonidas pressed the square head of the balsa wood bolt against his arm, his chest, his thigh. He tossed it lightly in the air and caught it again.

"*Endaxi*," he said grudgingly. "But—how you put in my back?"

"Like this," said Dave. "Hey, Marco—can you come here a minute?"

Dave picked up the pad and fastened it to Marco's shoulders, showing Leonidas the little hook hidden in the thick padding. He fixed one end of the wire to the hook and then walked away, carefully stretching out the fine wire so that it was taut and invisible. He reached the crossbow and fitted the wooden bolt into it. He put on his black gloves.

"Ready, Marco?" he called.

"Ready!" called Marco.

Leonidas watched apprehensively.

Dave released the bolt, which flew along the invisible wire and landed between Marco's shoulders. Marco fell to the ground, twitched, and lay still.

"Marco!" cried Leonidas, suddenly frightened.

Marco jumped up, grinning.

"Endaxi?" he asked.

Leonidas roared with laughter and relief.

"Endaxi!" he said. "Now—I try!"

Dave unfastened the bolt, wire and pad from Marco and fitted the pad on to Leonidas. Then he started to walk away towards the crossbow. Leonidas turned round to watch him, and got tangled up in the wire.

"Keep still, Leo!" shouted Dave. "Look towards the wall!"

Leonidas obediently turned towards the wall, wrapping the wire still tighter round himself. Marco darted in, spun Leonidas round, unwound the wire and kept Leonidas motionless until Dave reached the crossbow and fitted the wooden bolt into position.

"Endaxi, Leo?" he called.

"Endaxi!" shouted Leonidas.

He stood with his feet braced for the shock. The bolt came racing along the wire and nestled gently in his back. Leonidas looked over his shoulder, saw the bolt sticking out, and laughed.

"You're supposed to fall down when it hits you!" shouted Dave. "Oh, try it again, Leo. And this time, fall down and keep still until Karl tells you to get up."

"Quiet, please, rehearsal!" called Hal.

"*Prova!*" called Marco.

The rehearsal of the scene began.

Richard and Leonidas stood at the foot of the tower. They exchanged a few words, then Richard slipped off his cloak and handed it to Leonidas. He moved towards the tower buttress and Leonidas turned to watch him, his back towards the camera, which pulled back gently to include a pair of black-gloved hands resting on a loaded crossbow in the foreground of the picture. The gloved hands released the bolt. It flew away from the crossbow, raced along the invisible wire, and buried itself in Leonidas' back. Leonidas fell to the ground. Richard, unaware, was hurrying towards the buttress and disappearing behind it. As Richard disappeared, Yorky reached up and began to climb into shot. As he rose, the camera tilted up with him, and then panned to the right as he swung away from the tower and on to the wall. As the camera tilted up, Leonidas disappeared from the shot, but he dutifully kept still, face to the ground.

Everyone watched Yorky. Up and up he went, feeling for a hand-hold here, a foot-hold there. Once he slipped, and Stephen held his breath, not realizing that it was part of the act. Yorky found another hand-hold, hung there for a second, and then continued his climb up the grey stone wall. He was almost within reach of the battlements when he swung towards the final hand-hold, missed it, and fell, crashing down into the fall-boxes and disappearing behind the bushes. Dave and Hal raced towards him, with Richard leaping out from behind the buttress and running across the waste ground. The three of them helped Yorky to his feet. He was bruised but otherwise unhurt, and he was swearing furiously.

Leonidas, aware that something had gone wrong, sat up cautiously and looked around.

"What in hell happened?" shouted Karl.

"Don't know!" gasped Yorky. "Hand-hold—just not there! I'll have to go—up on the battlements—see what's happened —can't see—anything—from—down here!"

"OK, Yorky," said Hal. "Take your time."

Yorky moved away up the slope on the right and disappeared behind the wall. Everybody else relaxed, until Leonidas got up and walked away, forgetting that he was still attached to the crossbow by the wire. The crossbow crashed to the ground, and Marco dashed over to Leonidas and unhooked him before he could do any further damage. Dave the stunt man collected the bolt and the wire and replaced them on the crossbow. The other stunt men dragged away the fallboxes which had been crushed in Yorky's fall and replaced them with fresh ones. Stephen watched as Yorky appeared on the battlements and moved slowly along, leaning out at a dangerous angle and looking down at the place where the hand-hold should have been.

"H-how did Yorky g-get up there so quickly?" asked Stephen.

"There's a ladder on the other side," said Emma.

Yorky said nothing, but disappeared from the battlements and soon re-appeared below, coming down the slope towards the waiting group. He went straight to Karl.

"The hand-hold's gone," he said. "We'll have to get a new one fixed. It'll take some time."

"Ten minutes," said Karl.

"Half an hour," said Yorky.

They glared at each other.

"When it's fixed," said Yorky, "I'll want to try it out before we go for real. That is one big drop."

Karl looked at him. Then he looked up at the wall. Yorky was right—it was one big drop. Karl grunted.

"It's midday, Karl," said Hal. "Break for lunch while the job's being done?"

"Yes—break for lunch, Hal. But tell those goddam construction wops to move their asses."

"Lunch-break!" called Hal.

"Pausa—un' ora!" called Marco.

The unit was wrapping up when František the cameraman suddenly realized what was happening.

"Lunch-break!" he screamed. "What is this lunch-break? We have to wait an hour before we shoot? No, no! Look at the sun!"

Stephen was the only person foolish enough to do so. He found that it hurt his eyes.

"Already is midday!" shouted František. "A high wall like that—soon the sun will be on the other side! The wall will be in shadow! We must shoot now, now!"

Karl snapped at František, turned on his heel and walked away up the slope with Walther, disappearing behind the wall on his way to the barn for lunch. The unit trailed after him, taking the furious František with them.

As she left the set, Emma glanced up. High up on a ladder against the wall, a young Italian was beginning work on the new hand-hold. Yorky was issuing instructions from below, and Marco, holding the ladder, was translating them.

Richard was sitting in the director's chair, waiting.

Emma wondered what he was waiting for.

The barn, as usual, was hot and noisy. The straw matting at the sides kept out the sun, but Emma thought that it probably kept in the noise. Certainly once you were inside you couldn't hear sounds from outside.

Karl and Walther sat at a table in the middle of the barn with Brock, Ariadne and Leonidas, who were all in full costume and make-up. Brock, in black and silver, sat opposite Leonidas, who was bubbling over with excitement, waving his plum-coloured sleeves in the air as he described his adventure with the crossbow and tried to explain the mechanism of the wire to Ariadne, who was looking delectable in a shimmering gown of apple green.

On one side of them was the table with the stunt men, on the other side a table occupied by the still grumbling František and the camera crew. The sound crew shared a table with Hal and Emma. Beth Wardrobe, Babs Hairdressing and Charles Make-Up shared another table.

Somewhat to his surprise, Stephen found himself sharing a table with the company doctor and also with L. J. Hacker, who was a rare visitor to the set and did not care for the noisy camaraderie of the barn. Hacker had been a little uncertain of where he should sit—he felt that as the scriptwriter his position in the hierarchy entitled him to sit at Karl's table, but all the places there were already taken, and in any case he didn't really want to sit anywhere near Karl or Walther, who would address him as "Hack." But to sit, a silent stranger, at any of the tables filled with talkative technicians would have made him feel like an outcast. Then he caught sight of Stephen and the empty seat beside him, and homed in on it.

There was a tremendous noise with the clatter of pans and plates and cutlery and the chatter of over a hundred members of the unit. Electricians, painters, carpenters, drivers, extras—everybody was crowded together at the long tables, everybody was eating, drinking and talking. The only members of the unit who never ate in the barn were Richard and Yorky; they ate in Richard's trailer, which was parked in the shadiest spot that could be found.

František finished his lunch quickly and went over to Karl.

"I go back to the set," he said. "Soon the sun will be going."

"I'll come with you," said Walther. "What about you, Leonidas?"

Leonidas obediently rose and followed Walther and František out of the barn: The camera crew swallowed the last of their coffee and hurried after them. Beth Wardrobe, Babs Hairdressing and Charles Make-Up followed.

"Let's get going," said Gerry the Sound Recordist. "At least we'll get away from this infernal din."

The sound crew left.

Hal rose.

"I'll see if that hand-hold's OK," he said. "Don't you hurry, Emma. Karl's not moving yet. Can't shoot without him."

As Hal was going, a breathless stable-lad rushed past him and made for Marco, who listened to him briefly and then ran to catch Hal by the arm. He looked worried, but he kept his voice down.

"Hal, there is a fire in the stables!" he said. "The boy needs help to get the horses out to safety."

Hal swore under his breath.

"I'll get the stunt men," he said. "You go ahead. Do what you can."

Marco hurried out with the stable-lad and Hal moved quickly over to Dave's table.

"Listen," he said. "Don't move, anybody. I don't want the whole damned barn in a panic. There's a fire in the stables."

The stunt men made to rise, but Hal checked them.

"Walk up to the servery end. *Walk*, don't run. Duck out through the matting. Then run like hell for the stables and get those horses out!"

At a signal from Dave, the stunt men got up and walked through the barn towards the servery. They ducked out through the matting, letting it fall behind them so that nobody inside would get a glimpse of the burning stables. Once outside, they could smell the smoke and hear the horses squealing. They ran for the stables.

Hal was talking quietly to Karl, who clenched his fist and thumped the table softly several times. But even Karl didn't argue—a fire anywhere in the vicinity of horses took priority over everything. As long as the stunt men were on their own, they could get things under control. But if Karl moved, the whole unit would move. They would pour out of the barn, see the smoke, head for the stables, and, in trying to help, would create chaos.

"OK, Hal," said Karl. "I'll wait here till you get back."

He jerked his head contemptuously in the direction of the majority of the unit who were still sitting at the tables.

"As long as those S.O.B.'s see me sitting here they won't be in a hurry to get back to work. But get on the tails of those goddam stunt men, Hal. František's right—we ought to be shooting right now."

Karl turned and resumed his conversation with Brock and Ariadne.

Hal moved through the barn with long, unhurried strides. Emma watched him go towards the servery, lift the curtain of straw matting and step outside. Her heart went with him. She knew the danger. A flimsy makeshift stable. A lighted cigarette dropped in the straw. A wisp of smoke. And suddenly the whole place engulfed by flames. A frightened stable-lad running away. Horses, terrified of fire, plunging, rearing, kicking out at the men trying to lead them to safety. Black smoke choking them. Flames scorching them.

And in the middle of it all—Hal.

She fought down her feeling of panic. Fought down the feeling that she ought to be out there, helping. What help could she possibly be?

Walther and František would be getting agitated, wondering why Karl had not arrived. She had better go and break the news to them before they worked themselves into a lather of impatience.

She picked up her script, and as she rose she noticed that Dave had not gone out with the other stunt men. He was standing behind Karl.

For the first time she saw Karl Meister as an outsider might see him—a rather small man in his fifties. And Dave, standing behind Karl and leaning down now to speak to him—Dave was young and powerful.

Could Karl be in danger—from Dave, solid, familiar *Dave?*

But Hal had said, "Everybody will suspect everybody else. The whole damned unit will become hysterical."

She would not become hysterical.

She told herself firmly to stick to the job that she knew, and hurried off to tell Walther and František that shooting would have to be delayed even longer than anticipated.

As she expected, František exploded in a shower of fractured English.

"Yish-yish!" he shouted. "Is not possible to wait! The sun is going! The wall will be in shadow. We must shoot!"

Bob and Ernie, the camera crew, exchanged glances. They hoped that nobody would try to speak soothingly to František, which was the one thing guaranteed to inflame him to the point of spontaneous combustion. Walther, of course, did try to speak soothingly, and so he received the full force of František's desperate excitement. He soon gave in, not, Emma thought, unwillingly.

"OK, František, OK," he said. "Look—why don't we just go right ahead and shoot the scene?"

Everyone stared at him in astonishment. There was a very good reason why they should not go right ahead and shoot the scene: Karl was not there to direct it.

"The rehearsal before lunch was fine," said Walther. "Yorky, are you happy with that new hand-hold?"

"Why, yes, Walther, the hand-hold's OK, but—"

"Richard—are you OK to shoot?"

"Well, yes, Walther, I'm OK, but—"

"Right," said Walther. *"I'll* direct the scene."

Emma looked round hurriedly for some reason to stop him, and saw the crossbow.

"We can't shoot, Walther," she said. "Dave isn't here to fire the crossbow."

Walther went over and looked at the crossbow.

"No sweat," he said. *"I'll* fire it."

"You have to wear black gloves," said Emma desperately, and too late noticed that Dave's gloves were lying on the ground near the crossbow.

Walther put the gloves on.

"Come on, come on, let's get going!" he shouted. "Any minute now the sun will go and we'll have had it."

Any minute now, thought Emma, Karl will come and *you'll* have had it.

Why didn't Karl come?

For the first time since the picture began, she actually found herself wishing that Karl would arrive.

But Karl did not arrive.

And there was no Hal, no Marco.

Walther was in the driving seat, and he was going to make the most of his chance.

"Let's go!" said Walther. "Turn over!"

With a shrug, Bob switched on the camera.

"Speed up!" called Ernie.

The Clapper-Boy banged the clapper-board and darted out of shot.

"ACTION!" shouted Walther.

The scene began.

Richard gave his cloak to Leonidas and moved away towards the tower buttress. Leonidas turned his back towards the camera, watching Richard go. The camera tracked back to show Walther's black-gloved hands resting on the crossbow in the foreground. The hands moved, and the black bolt flew along the wire and buried itself in Leonidas' back. Leonidas fell. Richard dodged behind the buttress and was replaced by Yorky, who began his climb. The camera tilted up with him, losing Leonidas below on the ground. Everyone watched, holding their breath, as Yorky swung himself up the wall. The camera panned to the right with him. He slipped once, his deliberate slip designed to give the audience a thrill. He grasped another hand-hold and slowly made his way up and up until he reached out for the final hand-hold.

He seized it, hung motionless for a moment, and then swung himself up and over the battlements. He paused, and disappeared.

"Cut!" said Walther. "Cut and print it."

He was triumphant. He had successfully directed his first scene on *The Trumpets of Tuscany*.

Emma looked at him, and then looking past him she saw that Marco had arrived, smoke-stained and sweat-streaked, from the stables.

Yorky stood up on the battlements.

"OK, Walther?" he called.

"OK, Yorky," called Walther. "Got it in one! OK, Leonidas, you can get up now."

But Leonidas did not move.

Emma, suddenly frightened, left her post by the camera and ran towards him, just as Richard stepped out from behind the buttress. He too ran to Leonidas and knelt down beside him.

"My God!" he whispered. "My God—the bolt! It's gone clean through him!"

Emma knelt down and put out her hand to touch Leonidas, but drew it back again.

"He's dead!" she said incredulously. "Leonidas is dead!"

Richard suddenly jumped to his feet and ran away behind the tower. Emma could hear him retching, and felt sick herself. She knelt there, stunned, blood soaking into her skirt.

Everybody was struck still, frozen in the attitudes in which they realized what had happened—Ernie about to re-load the camera, Gerry the Sound Recordist taking off his headphones, František with his arms flung wide, Walther waving towards Yorky up on the battlements, Marco with his smoke-blackened hands to his mouth.

A sudden flash of green in the distance caught Emma's eye. Ariadne was coming down the slope, chatting gaily with Brock. Marco caught the horrified expression on Emma's face, turned, and saw Ariadne. Without a word he ran up the slope towards her. Emma could see him speaking quietly to Ariadne and Brock. Then he put his arm around Ariadne and led her gently away.

Brock came striding down the slope, his black and silver costume glinting in the sunlight, his great black cloak billowing round him like a thundercloud.

The stunt men arrived at a run, bringing with them the smell of horses and smoke. Their hands and faces were streaked with black, their eyes were red and streaming from the smoke. Among all the black leather costumes, one man in a blue sports shirt.

Hal.

Safe.

Emma closed her eyes and breathed a silent prayer of thanksgiving.

Behind Hal and the stunt men came Karl Meister and Dave.

They all stopped abruptly as they saw Leonidas lying on the ground with Brock standing over him and Emma kneeling beside him, while Walther and the rest of the crew stood motionless around the camera. Dave the stunt man moved forward, knelt beside Emma, looked at the bolt but did not touch it.

"It's the real one," he said slowly. "My God! That's not the trick bolt—it's the *real* one—you know what I mean . . ."

He looked up.

"What the hell happened?" he cried.

Everyone looked at Walther and his black-gloved hands.

"A mistake," said Walther. "An accident—could have happened to anybody—"

"No mistake!" said Dave harshly.

He stood up and strode back to Karl.

"The trick bolt was in position in the crossbow when we broke for lunch. I put it there myself, Karl. Somebody removed it and replaced it with the real bolt. This isn't an accident—it's plain bloody murder!"

Nobody moved.

Nobody spoke.

From the distant barn came the wailing of a sentimental song on the radio, while from the stables beyond the barn a slender plume of black smoke rose into the air and faded away.

All eyes were on Dave and Karl.

Brock sank to his knees beside Emma, and spoke in a whisper that only she could hear, although she knew that it was not to her that he was speaking.

It was to Leonidas, the young man who would never hear him, that Brock was whispering his valediction:

> "Fear no more the heat of the sun
>   Nor the furious winter's rages;
>   Thou thy worldly task hast done,
>   Home art gone, and ta'en thy wages:
>   Golden lads and girls all must,
>   As chimney-sweepers, come to dust."

11

The next few hours passed by Emma in a blur.

She remembered Brock taking off his great black cloak and draping it over Leonidas.

She remembered that Karl, incredibly, expected to continue shooting, and that Hal, shaking with rage, had refused, and had sent Marco to telephone the Production Office and the police.

People stood about aimlessly.

Policemen came and went.

The crew wrapped up their equipment, but remained on the set, smoking cigarettes, their eyes averted from the Wall of Death and the black thing below it. Emma had a vivid picture of Richard and Yorky sitting together on a fall-box near the tower, apart from all the rest, silent, waiting.

Somebody—she thought he must have been the Examining Magistrate—questioned her about the "accident." Why, he had asked, why had the real bolt been on the set, since they were only going to use the trick bolt in the scene? She remembered showing him the script, which called for a close shot of a real bolt piercing a real shield in a later scene. She would have expected the real bolt to have been kept safely in the Props room until it was needed, and couldn't say why it had been on the set. She must have answered all the questions, because the man went away, and she found herself once more sitting at her desk.

Later she was to find that she had automatically marked up her script and typed all her notes for the day. But her mind was not on any of these things. Round and round in her brain tramped the questions How? and Why? and Who?

At last she realized that she would get no peace until she had an answer to them.

She began to write them down, writing in shorthand because it was fast, almost as fast as she could think, but—even more important—because it was secret. What she was about to write was not for publication.

So she began:

Question: Accident—or murder?

Answer: Murder.

Question: Why are you so sure?

Answer: The harmless trick bolt had been used for rehearsals before lunch. Replacing it with the real bolt must have been deliberate. So it was murder.

Question: Why wasn't the scene shot before lunch?

Answer: Because a new hand-hold had to be made and tested.

Question: Why was the new hand-hold needed?

Answer: Because Yorky said that the original hand-hold had gone.

Question: Do you believe him?

Answer: I don't know.

Question: Do you think Yorky might have simply missed the original hand-hold during the rehearsal?

Answer: I cannot imagine a stunt double of Yorky's calibre making a mistake like that.

Question: Do you think somebody had tampered with the original hand-hold before the rehearsal?

Answer: It seems unlikely. Risky. They might have been seen doing it.

Question: Do you think Yorky deliberately missed the hand-hold, deliberately crashed all that way down on to the fall-boxes?

Answer: (*doubtfully*) Ye-es. I think he *must* have done. But even with mattresses and fall-boxes down below to break his fall, it would have taken a lot of nerve.

Question: But Yorky has a lot of nerve?

Answer: Yes.

Question: Why do you think he did it?

Answer: So that somebody would have a chance to switch the real bolt for the trick bolt while the unit was at lunch.

Question: Who was that somebody?

Answer: (*very slowly*) Yorky himself—or—could it be Richard?

Emma remembered Richard sitting in the director's chair, waiting, while Yorky gave instructions for the placing of the new hand-hold. Richard—in the director's chair—a few feet away from the crossbow with its harmless trick bolt. Nobody looking in his direction. And nearby—the Props box with the real bolt.

Her questioning continued.

Question: Why? Why should Richard do it?

Answer: Remember the look on Richard's face when he first saw Leonidas—young, beautiful, and a discovery of the Meister family? Didn't you think then that if looks could kill, Leonidas would be a dead man?

Question: I thought I was supposed to be asking the questions, not you. And here's the last one. What are you going to do about it?

Answer: I don't know. I'd like to have a closer look at that hand-hold—see if there really is only the new one that was fixed in the lunch-hour—or if there are two. If the original hand-hold is there, then Yorky had no need to call for a new one, and he staged that fall quite deliberately. And if Yorky staged the fall quite deliberately, it can only have been for one reason.

Question: And what is that reason?

Answer: To postpone the shooting of the scene until after the lunch-break, by which time the real bolt had been placed in the crossbow.

Question: So if there are two hand-holds on the wall—?

Answer: Yorky—or Richard and Yorky—murdered Leonidas.

The police had gone.

The great black cloak had gone.

Leonidas had gone.

Slowly the members of the unit came back to life, moved their equipment and cleared the set. Two stage-hands stood by Emma as she sat unseeing at her desk. She was the last person left.

"Permesso, signorina, lo scrittoio . . ."

She stood up.

"Oh, *scusi,*" she said.

She closed the typewriter, pushed her script and her shorthand notes into her bag. The two men removed the desk and the typing chair, and Emma followed them slowly up the slope and round to the other side of the wall. The heavy wooden ladder that Yorky used to climb to and from the battlements was still in place, resting against the tubular struts that supported the wall, the wall that from the outside looked like stone, but on the inside was rough timber and plaster and chicken wire. Emma trudged on, and then suddenly stopped.

The question about the two hand-holds was still stirring in her mind.

One hand-hold, and Yorky was in the clear.

Two hand-holds, and Yorky was, if not a murderer, then a murderer's accomplice.

But how long would the wall and the hand-holds remain as witnesses to that murder? The Art Department might come along at any minute to re-vamp the wall, taking away the saw-toothed battlements, re-painting the grey stone. And the hand-holds? Anything could happen to them.

Emma moved to the foot of the ladder and looked up.

She was terrified of heights . . .

She put her typewriter and bag down on the ground beside the ladder, grasped the thick wooden uprights, and began to climb.

She couldn't get a proper purchase, because the uprights were so thick and clumsy. It was like trying to wrap each hand around half a tree-trunk.

She climbed slowly and fearfully.

Each wooden rung was reinforced by a metal rung immediately beneath it, and sometimes her foot trod on the wooden rung, and sometimes she missed it and got her toes caught in the gap between the wood and the metal, so that she had to kick herself free.

She went on.

The wooden uprights were splashed with paint and plaster, and here and there they were cracked and splintered. She kept her eyes fixed on the paint-splashed wood and on the rough plasterwork of the wall beyond, and went on.

Her hands kept slipping on the clumsy uprights.

There was a nasty patch of splinters just above her right hand.

She paused for a moment.

Then she rested her hand on one of the wooden rungs. This was more comfortable than the broad spread of the upright. Safer, too, since she could wrap her hand over the rung and get a really good grip.

She put both hands on the rungs and went on climbing.

Her hands were wet with fear, and began to slip.

She paused to wipe her hands down the side of her skirt, and did the one thing she had been trying not to do.

She looked through the rungs straight down to the ground below.

Panic seized her.

She couldn't move.

She leaned her face against the hard wood and closed her eyes.

That was better.

Slowly the panic began to recede.

Still keeping her eyes closed, she began to climb blindly—right hand on rung, right foot on rung. Left hand on rung, left foot on rung. Pause and breathe.

Right hand up, right foot up, left hand up, left foot up.

Pause and breathe.

It was slow work, but she had found a rhythm, and it was taking her higher and higher.

Shouldn't be far to go now, she thought, but didn't dare open her eyes. She felt for the next rung with her right hand.

It was a double rung.

She felt along it, eyes still closed.

She felt above it for the next rung.

Another double.

There was some kind of cord wrapped round the wood. Cautiously she opened her eyes, and shut them again quickly.

A second ladder had been tied to the top of the first one, which was not tall enough to reach the walkway of planks at the top.

She paused, and then, still keeping her eyes tightly closed, went on climbing. She could manage the double rungs with her hands, but missed her footing several times.

Slowly she moved upwards.

Then her right hand grasped a single rung.

She must have climbed past the join, and must be on the second ladder now. A few more steps, and then her right foot was on a single rung. Then her left foot. Only single rungs now.

She must be near the top.

The knuckles of her right hand hit something hard.

Blindly she spread out her hand, and laid the palm along a piece of flat, rough wood. A plank.

Beyond it, another plank.

And another.

She had reached the level of the walkway behind the battlements.

So she was 40 feet above the ground, and she still had to swing herself off the ladder and on to the walkway.

She clung to the ladder. It suddenly felt like home.

But now there were no more rungs to haul herself up by. Somehow she had to nerve herself to scramble off the ladder. She half-opened her eyes and peeped through the lashes. There was a tubular strut coming up through a gap in the planking.

She put out her left hand, grasped the strut and flung herself forward on to the planks, crashing on to her knees.

Shaking with terror, sobbing for breath, eyes still tightly closed.

But she'd done it.

She was on the walkway.

Only 40 feet, and she felt as though she'd climbed Everest.

Yorky, and the stunt men, and the construction crew, they'd go up and down that ladder as if it were a staircase. It really wasn't difficult. Only—when you had no head for heights—terrifying.

She remembered telling Stephen that if Hal had told her to jump off the wall, she'd do it. It wasn't true. *Nothing* would make her jump.

Still clutching the strut, she opened her eyes.

Rough wooden planking beneath her, laid loosely over tubular horizontals. Rough timber and plaster in front of her—the inside of the battlements.

She still had to stand up and look over the other side to see how many hand-holds there were. Once more she wiped her sweating hands on her skirt and, holding on to the strut, hauled herself up on to her feet. The top of the strut was level with her waist, and she clung to it tightly. The saw-teeth of the battlements were level with her shoulders, and between each pair of teeth there was a gap. It was through one of these gaps that Yorky had swung himself up and over at the end of his climb. It was through one of these gaps that she must force herself to lean out and look down for the hand-holds.

She hooked her left hand round the top of the strut and, sick and trembling, forced herself to look out over the battlements.

Fear fell away from her.

The countryside spread out before her in a vast sheet of silvery-green olive groves. Here and there she could see the red-tiled roof of a farmhouse, and the squat grey bell-tower of an ancient abbey set about with dark cypresses and a neat walled garden. There was a cluster of roofs, big enough for a village. Beyond that, a single building big enough for a palace, a miniature Versailles, the patterns of its sandy walks and formal gardens clearly visible, a toy palace surrounded by a dark sea of trees and a pale foam of olive groves.

Beyond the palace, a shimmering lake blue as the sky. And far away, the city of Lucca, its tall arum-lily towers rising up within the corslet of its tree-crowned walls.

She could have shouted for joy. Glory hallelujah! *Gloria in excelsis Deo!*

Then she glanced down through the gap in the battlements and saw, quite plainly—two hand-holds.

Her elation vanished.

Well, she had found what she had come for.

A hand fell on her shoulder.

"Hi, Emma," said a familiar voice. "What brings you up here?"

It was Richard.

Sick and cold with fear, Emma forced herself to turn around and face him, even to smile at him. She put out her right hand and grasped the strut to steady herself. At least, by turning round she had forced Richard to take his hand off her shoulder. But, oh God, why was she such a fool as to come up here? Richard must realize that she was suspicious about those hand-holds. If he and Yorky had killed Leonidas, he would have no hesitation in killing again to keep her quiet. And everyone would think it was an accident—Emma, falling off a wall where she had no business to be in the first place.

It would be so easy for him to push her off the walkway—easier perhaps than he could guess, for her legs were still shaky after she'd made herself climb that ladder. All the same, she was determined to make a fight of it, however feeble. She could still shout for help. But could she? Her mouth was dry, her throat was tight—she would probably squeak like a frightened rabbit.

"It's a beautiful view," she said, and was surprised to find that her voice sounded quite normal.

Richard looked out over the olive-trees towards Lucca.

"Great little place, that," he said. "Been there hundreds of years. But all those damned towers—they look just like tombstones . . ."

Emma shivered.

But—keep him talking, she thought. Keep him talking, keep an eye on him—and keep another eye out for anybody moving down below, and if you see someone, yell for help. But what do you talk about to a man you suspect of murder? Her glance fell on the rough timber supports of the battlements. Wood . . . an actor . . . a wooden actor . . .

"Did you ever read *Pinocchio?*" she asked. "The boy carved out of a piece of wood?"

(Richard must think her mad!)

"No, I never read it," said Richard. "Saw the movie, though." He hummed one of the tunes. " 'Hi-diddle-de-dee, an actor's life for me . . .' Poor boy! He thought it would be great to be an actor. Well, he found out the hard way . . ."

Overlooking the very place where Leonidas had been killed only a few hours ago, was Richard talking about Pinocchio—*or Leonidas?*

"The man who wrote Pinocchio came from near here," said

Emma, blundering on desperately, unable to stop. "He came from a little place called . . . called . . . Collodi." The name suddenly surfaced from the depths of her memory. "I've forgotten what his real name was, but when he wrote the book he called himself Carlo Collodi, after his home-town."

This was absolutely crazy. Making polite conversation with a man who's just waiting to kill you.

"I'll be darned," said Richard. "Where's the place he came from?"

Emma turned away from him to look towards Lucca. She still gripped the strut with her right hand, but with the other she pointed vaguely in the direction of the village. She had no idea where Collodi was—in fact, up until a few seconds ago she didn't even know that she knew the name of the place—but she felt that its exact location was of no great importance at the moment.

"You didn't come all the way up here just to look at the place where the Pinocchio man came from, did you?" asked Richard.

What reason could she possibly give? Her brain raced frantically. All she could think of was olive groves.

"Olive groves," she said, and then she had it. "I—I wondered if I'd be able to see the villa where Karl and Walther are staying—it has some olive groves, and we're supposed to be going to film there some time. But I suppose looking for one particular olive grove around Lucca is like looking for a needle in a haystack."

"I don't know about the olive grove," said Richard, "but you can certainly see the villa from here—it's that quiet little number that looks like a summer cottage for the Vanderbilts."

"What—the toy palace?" she said, genuinely astonished.

Richard chuckled.

"Toy palace, yes, indeedy," he said.

She felt one of the loose planks move suddenly under her feet. Someone had stepped on it. She stiffened, and tightened her grip on the strut. Then she realized that it wasn't Richard who had trodden on the plank. Richard hadn't moved. He was still looking in the direction of the toy palace. Somebody else was moving about on the walkway. One of the stunt men? One of the construction crew? She would shout for him to come and save her.

She swung round to greet her unknown rescuer.

Yorky . . .

Cold fear crawled over her again.

Richard on one side of her, Yorky on the other, a walkway of loose planks only a yard wide, and a drop of 40 feet beneath her.

She tried to smile, and felt that she must be grinning like a death's head.

Her teeth clenched together.

"Hi, Emma," said Yorky. "Have you come to admire the view?"

She nodded, speechless with fright.

"Has Richard shown you the place we're living in?" said Yorky. "See that farmhouse with the red roof? That's it."

She turned slightly, pretending to look towards the farmhouse, and as she did so, she saw Richard and Yorky exchange a quick glance.

"Emma! Emma!"

Somebody down below was calling her name. Somebody walking towards the ladder. Marco. He must have noticed her bag and typewriter there.

She forced her teeth to unclench.

"Marco!" she cried desperately.

Marco looked up.

"What is it, Marco?" called Richard.

"Mr. Meister wants Emma," called Marco.

She was safe.

They wouldn't dare do anything now, not with Marco as a witness. She turned towards the ladder, and looked straight down to the ground.

Panic returned.

She clung to the strut. She couldn't move.

"Here, let me give you a hand, Emma," said Richard. "I'll go down first, and Yorky will help you on to the ladder."

Richard swung himself easily on to the ladder, moved down a few rungs, and waited for her.

Yorky helped her on to the ladder, and held her wrists until she had a good grip on the top rung. She wondered what he would have done if Marco had not arrived . . .

"You're quite safe," said Yorky. "Richard is only a few steps below you. Just take it gently, one step at a time."

She took it gently, one step at a time. Panic faded. Her right foot struck the double rung, and she felt as though she was meeting an old friend. She climbed on down past the double ladder, and suddenly she was down, and safely on the ground, and there was Marco waiting for her.

"Thanks very much, Richard," she said.

"You're welcome," said Richard. "Coming, Yorky?"

"Coming," said Yorky.

He descended the ladder at speed.

"Marco, is it OK for us to leave the location now?" asked Richard.

"Yes, the police are letting everyone go home," said Marco. "I do not know what will happen tomorrow, but the Production Office will telephone you later this evening."

"*Ciao,* Marco," said Richard and Yorky, and moved away towards the car park. Emma noticed that Richard was humming the tune from *Pinocchio* again.

"*Ciao,*" said Marco.

He picked up Emma's typewriter and walked with her towards the barn.

"But, Emma, you are shaking," he said suddenly. "What is the matter?"

"No head for heights," said Emma truthfully.

"But I have seen you climb ladders higher than that before now," he said.

"Yes—with the camera crew all round me," said Emma. "It's not so bad then. This time I went up on my own."

"But why did you want to go up there on the battlements?" he asked.

"I wanted to see if there were two hand-holds or only one," she said. She was still trembling, and her jaw ached from clenching her teeth together so tightly.

"*Cretina!*" said Marco affectionately. "No need for you to climb ladders. I could have told you. Two hand-holds. There was one far over on the right, and when Yorky was rehearsing the climb he missed it. So he made a great fuss and said there was no hand-hold, so we had to fix another one for him, not quite so far for him to stretch. I was there, translating his instructions for Aldo. Why are you suddenly so interested in hand-holds?"

"Marco," said Emma, "why do you think Yorky wanted a second hand-hold?"

"Because he found the first hand-hold was too far for him to reach," said Marco. "Perhaps Yorky is getting old and can no longer make such big leaps."

Marco grinned with the carefree malice of youth which knows that it will never grow old.

"Do you really think that?" asked Emma.

"What are you trying to say, Emma?" he asked.

"I think," said Emma, "that Yorky missed the hand-hold deliberately."

"But why?" said Marco. "It was a big drop—and in front of everybody, too."

"I think that was the idea," said Emma. "Everybody saw him fall, and everybody understood that a new hand-hold must be made. And then everybody left the set—except you and Aldo and Richard and Yorky."

"So?" said Marco.

"You and Aldo were facing the wall, and Yorky was calling the instructions from behind you?"

"Yes."

"Marco, what was Richard doing?"

Marco stared at her.

"He was sitting and waiting for Yorky," he said.

"If he had changed the trick bolt for the real bolt, would you or Aldo have noticed?"

Marco stopped dead, staring at the ground.

At last he said, "I do not think either of us would have noticed. We were concentrating on getting the work done. And we were facing the wall at the time. But it would have been a very risky thing for Richard to do. Either of us might have turned round at any time."

"But you did not turn round?"

"No."

"When you had finished the job, did you all leave together?"

Marco thought for a moment.

"No," he said. "I helped Aldo carry away the ladder. When we left, Richard was still sitting in Karl's chair, and Yorky was standing talking to him."

"And Karl's chair was close to the crossbow, and close to the Props box with the real bolt?"

"Yes. That would have been the best time to change the bolts, I suppose. But why—why should Richard or Yorky have wanted to kill Leonidas?"

"Just now," said Emma, "you were amused at the thought of Yorky getting old—you thought he'd missed the hand-hold because his strength had failed him."

Marco looked a little ashamed.

"I did not mean to be cruel," he murmured.

"How do you think Richard felt at having to play scenes with someone as young and handsome as Leo?" demanded Emma. "When you think of the films Richard has been in recently, he has never had to face any competition. He has always been the handsome athletic hero, and when he has had a sidekick, it has always been a comic character, a foil to help him to shine brightly. Now thanks to Walther, Richard's sidekick is younger, stronger and even more handsome than Richard himself. Leo made Richard look old. You know the film business, Marco."

"Yes," said Marco. "It would not be the first time that the studio bosses have thrown the star off their pay-roll because he looked too old."

"And it wouldn't just be curtains for Richard," said Emma. "It would be curtains for Yorky as well. He's been so long with Richard."

"Then you think they were in it together?" he asked.

"Yes," said Emma. "Richard and Yorky are so close they'd have to be in it together."

"But, Emma—you were up on the battlements with both of them just now! If you are right, that was a dangerous thing to do! Do you think they suspected why you were up there, and what you were looking for?"

"I don't know," said Emma. "But if they killed Leonidas, they must have suspected something. I thought they were going to kill me and pretend it was an accident. I can't tell you how glad I was to hear you calling for me! Good heavens, I'd quite forgotten! Didn't you say Karl wanted me?"

"Accidenti!" said Marco. "I had forgotten too. Yes, he wants to give you some script changes."

Emma found Karl and Walther seated at a table in the deserted barn with only Dave the stunt man in attendance. Outside, there was the noise and bustle of the unit wrapping up, loading equipment on to trucks and cars, and pulling out. Inside, behind the servery partition, the kitchen staff were clattering pots and pans and crockery, shouting instructions to each other, quarrelling and joking, all against a background of music squawking from the badly tuned radio. But around Karl's table there seemed to be a wall of silence. Karl was turning the pages of his script, while Walther smoked a cheroot and made occasional scribbles on the back of an old envelope.

"Emma," said Karl, "I'm having to make some changes in the script. How many scenes do we still have to do with Leonidas?"

Emma flinched, then took a deep breath and sat down at the table. She opened her script, and when she spoke her voice was as steady as Karl's.

"Scene 72," she said.

Karl riffled through his script and found scene 72.

"Scrub it," he said.

"Scenes 120 to 130 inclusive," said Emma.

Karl looked at them.

"We'll have to play them with a double for Leonidas," he said.

"And scenes 131 to 135 inclusive," said Emma. "That's the lot."

Karl looked at them for several minutes.

"The Hack will have to re-write them," he said.

Karl closed his script. He sighed, and looked straight at Emma. His face was sombre.

"Leonidas was a good kid," he said. "Walther discovered him—did you know that? We had plans for him—and Ariadne. Next year maybe . . . and now here I am cutting him out of the script . . ."

Walther looked up from his envelope.

"Poor little girl," he said huskily. "Alone in the world . . ."

An incredible thought flashed through Emma's mind, and was immediately suppressed. Walther was old enough to be Ariadne's father, possibly even her grandfather.

Karl nodded his head at Emma to signify that she could go. As she rose, he frowned.

"What's that goddam mess on your skirt, Emma?" he said.

Emma looked down at her skirt. The front was stiff and brown with dried blood.

"Leonidas . . ." she said faintly, and Karl jerked back his head as though she had struck him.

With a sob, Emma turned and ran out of the barn.

At last the dreadful day was over, and Emma found herself in the car with Hal, returning to Lucca through the pale green of the gathering twilight. Emma, tired and dishevelled, her skirt stained with blood, her bare arms scratched and grubby from her climb up to the battlements, Hal with his clothes still smelling of smoke and horses. The smell reminded Emma of something that had been puzzling her.

"How did you get the stable fire under control so quickly?" she asked.

"It wasn't a fire," said Hal shortly.

"But, Hal, I saw the smoke—"

"That's all it was. Smoke. Some joker pinched a smoke-pot from the Props room. He let it off inside the stables. Stable-lad panicked."

"He'd probably never seen a smoke-pot before," said Emma. "He wouldn't know that it was harmless. A canister belching black smoke does look a bit frightening."

"The place was full of smoke," said Hal. "By the time we got there the horses were terrified. We had a job to get them out. But there was no fire. Then—Leonidas—with that damned bolt shot through him . . ."

He rested his thumb on his cheekbone and rubbed his fingertips over his closed eyelids, as though trying to wipe out the memory. They were both silent for a while.

At last Emma said, "It strikes me, Hal, that the hoax with the smoke-pot was horribly well-timed. None of us on the set noticed that the bolt was the real one, but it wouldn't have deceived any of the stunt men if they'd had to fire it. But because of that smoke-pot business, there weren't any stunt men on the set."

"No," said Hal. "They were all with me. In the stables."

"Not quite all of them," said Emma reluctantly. "Dave wasn't with you, was he?"

"Dave was on duty," said Hal. "Standing guard over Karl."

On guard! Emma felt a great weight lifted from her.

"I may as well tell you," said Hal, "but don't spread it around. The Commissario in Venice said he thought the poison that killed Stella Camay might have been intended for Karl."

(So Stephen's guess had been right. The wrong person had been killed.)

"I've had Dave and Johnny on duty ever since. Unofficial bodyguards for Karl. They live at the villa with him and Walther. One or other stays with him all the time. Karl only eats what everybody eats. No lunch-boxes put aside for him. No special dishes at the villa . . ."

"Oh, I'm so glad about Dave!" said Emma. "I was afraid—I mean—I almost thought—"

"Dave's OK," said Hal. "He and I both thought the trouble in the stable might be designed to draw the stunt men away. We took it for granted that the target was Karl. We never dreamed it was Leonidas . . ."

Emma wondered if she dared mention her theory about Richard and Yorky, and her discovery of the two hand-holds. But Marco had already known about the two hand-holds without her help, so perhaps Hal knew it too.

"And, Emma—no detective stuff! If you can suspect Dave, you'd suspect the Angel Gabriel. Stick to Continuity, there's a good girl . . ."

12

The police sealed off La Rocca for their investigations and the crew, with nowhere to work, mooched around Lucca or sat gloomily in their hotels. From time to time people were called to the Questura for further questioning. Walther was the chief suspect, since he had actually fired the fatal bolt, but the more the police saw of him the less they believed him to be capable of murder.

"Frank, what's happened about that idiot of a Props man?" asked Hal.

"Sacked," said Frank Jones. "The Rome office is sending us a replacement. He actually had the nerve to ask me for a reference because he's got six children! I pointed out to him that because he hadn't taken proper care of the smoke-pots, somebody was able to start a scare in the stables, and because he hadn't taken proper care of a dangerous weapon, meaning the real bolt, somebody was able to kill Leonidas."

"What did he say?" asked Emma.

"He still wanted a reference," said Frank Jones.

"And what did you do?"

"Oh, I gave him one. This is Italy, after all."

Emma and Marco smiled, but Hal did not.

"Give him a reference, give him a kick up the arse!" he growled. "If he'd done his job properly, Leonidas would be alive today. Marco—when the new man comes, put the fear of God into him!"

Marco smiled.

"I will do better than that," he said. "I will put the fear of the *Bisteccone* into him."

"Meaning me?" said Hal.

"Yes," said Marco. "You see, *Bisteccone* means—it means 'the big Englishman.' "

He shot a quick glance at Emma and saw that she approved of his tactful translation.

Walther returned from the Questura. The police called in Hal and Dave the stunt man, then Yorky, and then Richard Traherne.

"Marco, do you think the police will question Richard about the two hand-holds?" said Emma.

"A famous American film star like Richard Traherne?" said Marco. He smiled. "No, they will not ask him any unpleasant questions. They will all be wanting to have themselves photographed with him."

After a few days in the doldrums, Karl galvanized everybody into action by announcing that shooting would begin immediately at the villa of the American contessa. Emma suspected that Karl had no clear plan of action, but had simply made up his mind to shoot something—anything—rather than allow the crew to become utterly demoralized. The next day everybody, apart from Ariadne, was working again.

The estate of the American contessa, the "toy palace" that Emma had seen from the battlements, was a complete contrast to the barren hill-top of La Rocca. It was a smiling countryside of woods and olive groves, vineyards and wheatfields, and Karl filmed the stunt men riding through all of them. Sometimes they were led by Brock, in which case they wore black leather costumes and rode black horses. Sometimes they were led by Richard, and then they wore his colours of green and gold, and they rode chestnut horses. Emma did her best to keep clear of Richard, and took care never to be alone when he was on the set.

Nobody knew what scenes Karl proposed to shoot at the villa, so Emma tackled him about it. He fished a cigarette packet out of his pocket and looked at some notes scribbled on it.

"The other day," he said, "I went into the cathedral at Lucca and I saw a tomb of a girl called Ilaria. She's lying on a white couch, and looks as if she's just fallen asleep. I want to do a shot of Ariadne looking just like that. Dressed in a white robe, with a long white cloak . . ."

"But how—" began Emma.

"Don't ask me how it's going to fit into the script, Emma, because I don't know yet. I'm playing all this by ear—hell, what else can I do, when I don't know how soon the goddam police are going to let us go back to La Rocca? But this place is full of production value, and I'm going to milk it for all it's worth. Come and see."

He took her down an avenue of cypress trees to a classical villa of pale stone, set among formal gardens.

"This is where Walther and I are staying," he said. "My room overlooks the gardens."

Karl led the way to a terrace, and Emma found herself looking down over a series of gardens, where low hedges were clipped into geometric patterns round bright flowerbeds, and where trees were shaped like corkscrews, or drums, or pyramids, or pineapples—anything so long as it was not remotely tree-shaped. Together they went down a shady tunnel made from trees bent into hoops, and came to a water-garden presided over by two stone river-gods, reclining back to back like a pair of outsize book-ends. It was the kind of location that dreams are made of.

Within a few hours the whole place had been converted into a film studio. One of the out-buildings housed Wardrobe, another Hairdressing, and another Make-Up. Another held the electricians' gear, and another had become the Props room. Emma saw Marco talking earnestly to the new Props man, and gathered that he was instilling the fear of the *Bisteccone* into him.

The next morning Ariadne returned to work for the first time since the death of Leonidas. Marco accompanied her to the location, and handed her over to Beth Wardrobe, Babs Hairdresser and Charles Make-Up, who surrounded her with silent sympathy. She was quiet and composed, but Emma could see that she was under a great strain.

One of the first shots they made in the gardens was of Ariadne standing in the sunlight beside a fountain that splashed drops of sparkling water on her upturned face. Then there were shots of Ariadne walking demurely down the tunnel of trees towards the stone river-gods, Ariadne watching a family of swans in the water-gardens, Ariadne with a pretty little white pony eating out of her hand.

At the end of the day Marco accompanied Ariadne to her hotel in Lucca.

"She says that she is glad to be back at work," he said to Emma the next morning. "It gives her something else to think about."

They filmed in an old, walled garden, where flowers spilled out of terracotta jars big enough for Ali Baba. Ariadne sat dreaming beside a dovecote in the June sunshine. Then, as though hearing Richard's voice somewhere in the distance, she rose and went running through the garden, with a cloud of silver-white doves wheeling round her.

It was a hot day, and when the shot was over, Marco gathered a handful of fallen feathers from the dovecote and made them into a miniature fan for Ariadne.

Then came the lunch-break.

Meals at the villa were eaten al fresco, in a flagged courtyard shaded by a trellis of vines. Ariadne carried the little fan of feathers, but she needed both hands to manage her long skirt, and by the time she reached the courtyard only one feather remained, and she dropped it on to the table beside her plate. She and Brock were seated at Karl's table, Brock magnificent in black velvet slashed with white, and Ariadne fragile in a dress of pale green, her hair loose save for a single plait wound round her forehead like a golden circlet. Dave the stunt man, still acting as Karl's bodyguard, sat at one end of the table, and script-writer L. J. Hacker sat at the other. Karl beckoned to Emma and Stephen to join him. As they sat down, Walther leaned across the table, picked up the silvery feather beside Ariadne's plate, and stuck it upright into the golden braid around her forehead.

"Minnehaha, Laughing Water!" said Walther. And he laughed.

What a fool the man was, Emma thought, and was about to start eating when Karl brought his fist crashing down on to the rough wooden table in sudden excitement.

"That's it!" he cried. "You've got it, Walther! Minnehaha, Laughing Water! You remember when we saw *Hiawatha*—oh, years ago, long before the war, some big place in London. We were up very high, looking down to some kind of circus arena way below—filled with Indian braves and squaws singing and dancing—real crappy stuff—and then they came to the Death of Minnehaha . . . she was all in white, with a great white cloak . . . like that girl Ilaria in the cathedral—and they put her on a white bier and lifted her up high and carried her away in a great funeral procession—and the snow was falling . . ."

"Good Lord," said Hacker softly, "I saw that too. *Hiawatha* at the Albert Hall. I was a schoolboy then, and I don't remember much about it . . . but I do remember the Death of Minnehaha . . ."

He was silent, thinking back over the years to the scene that had so moved him. Then he woke up.

"But Karl—how does Minnehaha fit in with *Trumpets of Tuscany?*"

"You're the script-writer, Hack," said Karl. "You sort something out . . ."

Lunch continued, and Emma noticed that Hacker took no part in the conversation going on all around him. He twisted his glass of wine round and round in his hands, and then held it still and stared into it as though he was hypnotized. Lunch had reached the coffee stage when Hacker at last came out of his trance.

"Karl," he said slowly, "how would it be if we used the old Romeo and Juliet potion trick—say Ariadne has to sham dead to escape from Brock, and they carry her in a great funeral procession . . ."

Karl thought about it.

"A funeral procession—everyone in black—with Ariadne asleep in a long white cloak . . ." he said.

"And . . . and a black-draped barge on a river," said Hacker. "They put Ariadne into it, and a black-clad ferryman stands at the prow and poles the boat away into . . . into the sunset . . ."

"And then Richard finds her and kisses her awake—just like the Sleeping Beauty!" cried Karl. "Great! You work out the details, Hack, and let me have it this evening."

"And what am I doing all this time?" asked Brock.

"You—you hear that Ariadne has died," said Hacker, improvising hastily. "You suspect a trick, and you want to see for yourself. You dash off on your horse. And then—you see the procession—you rein in your horse—you see Ariadne—perhaps you even touch her hand and find that it is cold . . ."

" 'Cold, cold, my girl,' " said Brock.

He thought for a moment.

"Do I get off my horse?" he asked. "Oh yes, of course—I dismount and kneel reverently on the ground."

"You are a broken man," said Hacker.

Brock's face crumpled and his eyes glazed over.

"The procession moves away and leaves you kneeling," said Hacker.

Brock, slumped at the table, watched the procession moving away.

"We stay with the procession," said Karl. "We take it through the fields, and along by a lake—we'll see the whole procession reflected in the water—and along an avenue of cypresses—and then we come to the river and put Ariadne into the barge, and the snow is falling soft . . ."

He caught Emma's eye.

"Hell!" he said. "It's summertime! We can't have any goddam snow!"

His hobgoblin face looked as tragic as Brock's.

He was quite right. The countryside was at high summer. June. But it was the falling snow that had made the Death of Minnehaha so memorable.

"What about white rose-petals?" said Emma suddenly. "Or a pear-tree? It may not be quite the right month for it—but—well, white blossom of some kind . . ."

"A tree—some kind of tree by the river's edge," said Karl excitedly. "Hanging over the black barge and scattering white petals over Ariadne and the ferryman—"

"It would be nice if we could have some mourning women in the barge," said Hacker dreamily. "Like the queens in the *Morte d'Arthur*—they sit motionless and the white blossoms snow down on them . . . and then the ferryman rows away into the sunset . . . and then . . ." His eyes sparkled. "I've got it! Then one of the mourning women puts back her veil, and we see that it's—"

"It's Richard!" shouted Karl. "Of course! And the other veiled women are his men, and they bring out some oars and start to row . . . and then Richard does the Sleeping Beauty bit and wakes Ariadne . . ."

"And what about me?" said Brock, who was no longer a broken man but a distinctly star actor. "Don't I find out that it was a trick and—and beat the hell out of somebody?"

"How would it be," said Hacker, feeling his way cautiously, "if Brock were to—wait a minute—this black procession—it's all priests and monks, isn't it?"

"Could be," said Karl.

"Well, when Brock finds out he's been tricked," said

Hacker, "he and his men attack the monastery where the monks and priests are living—"

"Great!" said Karl. "Attack at night—kill the priests—set the place on fire—smoke and flames—" He turned to Dave. "And lots of fighting, Dave!" he said.

Dave grinned. The stunt men would enjoy that far more than the rest of the story so far. He knew who'd have to carry Ariadne on the bier for miles and miles in the blazing sun—unless he could talk Karl into using an ox-cart for the job—*and* who'd have to row the heavy barge into the sunset—not Hacker and Karl who dreamed up the idea, but the poor bloody stunt men.

"Where are you going to shoot all this monastery stuff, Karl?" asked Walther.

"At La Rocca," said Karl. "As soon as the police let us back there, Luciano can re-vamp the castle into a monastery—no sweat. Right—back to work everybody!"

As Ariadne rose to go, she took the feather out of her hair and dropped it on the table. Everyone except Stephen returned to the set, but he continued to sit there, looking at the feather gleaming in the sunshine. He had listened in silent amazement as Hacker and Karl had built up a complete sequence, brick by brick, until it all seemed solid and somehow inevitable. A sequence that would involve the three stars of the film, all the stunt men, a procession of at least a hundred people, and the re-building of a castle into a monastery. And all out of something as light and as insubstantial as a feather. Even as he watched, a little puff of air lifted the silver feather and floated it away across the courtyard.

A hundred local people were engaged to walk in the Minnehaha procession. Costumes for them were hired from Rome. For Ariadne, Beth Wardrobe made a fabulous white cloak lined with swansdown, fit for a Snow Princess. Luciano the Art Director designed a tree which would release a snowstorm of white blossom on the black-draped barge.

As the days went by, Ariadne lost the look of strain which had been so noticeable, and was once more absorbed into the busy life of the unit.

There were the usual hold-ups and delays, including several summer thunderstorms which sent the funeral procession scurrying for cover and ruined thousands of Luciano's artificial petals.

But the Minnehaha procession took place.

The slight, still figure of Ariadne, enfolded in the cloak of white swansdown, hands crossed over a white lily on her breast, was borne high on a white bier drawn by a team of white oxen. Black-clad monks and priests accompanied her, walking slowly across fields, then under the silvery-grey olive trees, and then beside a lake where they were mirrored in the smooth water.

They were intercepted by a furious Brock galloping towards them. He demanded to see Ariadne, to touch her hand; and he found that she was as cold as death.

Shocked, he dismounted from his horse and knelt reverently, a broken man.

The procession continued slowly down the avenue of cypresses, the white figure of Ariadne floating against the dark background.

It reached the river bank, where the black barge was moored, a single ferryman waiting in the bows, and four black-veiled women sitting round a black catafalque.

At a signal from Karl, Ariadne was laid in the barge, dazzling white at the centre of the blackness.

At another signal from Karl, Luciano's tree sent drifts of white blossom fluttering down into the barge to cover Ariadne and the mourning women.

The ferryman slowly poled the barge away down the river and out of sight round a bend.

One of the mourning women threw off her veil. It was Richard.

The other mourners followed suit. They fitted oars to the boat and pulled swiftly. They reached a small bay and ran the boat ashore. Richard tore off his black cloak, stooped over the sleeping Ariadne and kissed her awake.

Richard was not on call until the end of the sequence, when he threw off the veil. He made no approach to Emma, but she felt easier when his scenes were completed and he and Yorky returned once more to the farmhouse.

Marco still accompanied Ariadne to and from the location every day, and before long Beth Wardrobe and Babs Hairdresser began to scent a romance. They kept their thoughts to themselves until one day they were walking with Emma along the high walls of Lucca, and there were no other members of the unit around to overhear them. It was a Sunday, when the young people paraded in their best clothes, and naturally the conversation turned to Marco and Ariadne.

"She relies on him an awful lot," said Beth. "It's always 'Marco will know,' or 'I will ask Marco about that,' isn't it?"

"Leonidas used to say exactly the same," said Babs.

"Well, Marco was their friend before the picture started," said Emma. "It's only natural that Ariadne should turn to him."

"It's pretty clear that he's in love with her," said Beth.

"Oh, but surely—" began Emma, and stopped. It had never occurred to her that Marco might be in love—she had always thought of him as being totally dedicated to his work. But Hal thought that Emma was dedicated to *her* work, and if Hal could be wrong about Emma, then Emma might well be wrong about Marco.

"Marco's a nice lad," said Babs. "I wouldn't mind him myself . . ."

"Mmm, if I were in Ariadne's shoes I wouldn't turn him down," said Beth.

"But Leonidas died only a few weeks ago!" said Emma. She found the conversation distasteful.

"I know that," said Beth, "and of course Marco is no Leonidas, but what's going to happen to Ariadne when the picture finishes? Karl and Walther will go back to Hollywood, Marco will go back to Rome, and Cinderella will go back to sweeping up the cinders, or whatever she was doing before she married Leonidas."

A few days later Ariadne was sitting beside Emma's desk, and Marco was kneeling at her feet. The pearl embroidery on her costume had broken, and Marco was picking up the pearls and returning them to her one by one, while Ariadne was feeding him with grapes, one for every pearl, and giggling like a schoolgirl. Emma felt that perhaps Babs and Beth were right, and that Marco was indeed in love.

Smack!

A small missile hit the front of Emma's desk and fell to the ground. Surprised, she looked up, and saw Walther.

"Marco!" he shouted. "Gimme a fresh pack—and move it!"

He snapped his fingers.

Emma saw that the missile was an empty cheroot packet. She looked at Marco as he scrambled to his feet, fists clenched, his face furious, his whole body tense. But before Marco could move, Hal strode in from nowhere, picked up the packet and made straight for Walther. He spoke to him very quietly, and Walther reddened and walked away. Hal moved off in another direction, taking care not to look at Marco for fear of spoiling *la bella figura*. But the damage had been done, and the light-hearted atmosphere had been shattered.

I could *kill* Walther! thought Emma.

They returned to work in the olive groves, a charming picture of Ariadne riding down the dusty, sun-dappled track under the twisted trees, her red-gold hair floating loose in the breeze and her little white pony jingling the golden bells on its harness.

At the end of the day's shooting, Walther announced that the American contessa had invited Ariadne to stay at the villa for the duration of the film. She would no longer be staying at the hotel in Lucca, and so she would no longer need Marco to accompany her to and from the location. The Meister family was protecting its property.

Shooting continued, and Emma realized with something of a shock that it was almost the end of June, and soon they would be plunged into the excitement of filming the Palio at Siena. Karl called a production meeting round the lunch-table under the olive-trees. Hal and Marco were there, Emma, Stephen and L. J. Hacker. Frank Jones the Production Manager sat on one side of Karl, Walther sat on the other. Dave the stunt man, on duty as Karl's bodyguard, sat next to Hal. The arrangements for filming the Palio were well in hand.

"When do the extra camera crews arrive, Frank?" asked Karl.

"July 1st," said Frank Jones. "They'll stay the night at Lucca and then travel to Siena the next day with the main unit. You will all get to Siena at nine A.M. The parade doesn't start until the afternoon, but you've got to stake your claim to your camera positions before the crowds arrive. You'll have an early lunch, get back to your positions and be prepared to stay there until the Palio is over. From what I can make out, you'll be jammed solid until the race is over at about seven o'clock."

"Right," said Karl. "I'll be with the first camera. We shall cover the entry of the parade and the start of the race. You'll be with me, Emma. You too, Hal."

"You too, Dave," said Hal. He wasn't relaxing his precautions for Karl's safety. A tightly packed, wildly excited crowd would provide excellent cover for a killer.

"Walther will be directing the second unit," said Karl. "They'll be opposite the bell-tower. They should get some good shots of the parade, and of the horses falling as they come down the slope. Third and fourth units—they'll be the new crews—they'll cover the middle and end of the parade and of the race. Now, Frank, we'll have four units at different points. The centre of the Campo will be packed with people, and each camera will be penned in by the crowd. How do we keep in touch with each other? Walkie-talkies?"

"No," said Frank Jones. "Walkie-talkies are out—you'd never hear with all the racket going on. The best way to maintain contact is for you to have some messengers who can move about on the race-track itself, like the official stewards and marshals—most of those will be in mediaeval costume, so our people can do the same. Wardrobe are fixing up Hal and Marco with black and white harlequin tunics and hose—the outfits that Brock's indoor servants wear. Luckily for us, black and white are the colours of the City of Siena, so there'll be plenty of people wearing similar costumes. Perfect camouflage."

"I need two more messengers," said Hal.

He looked round the table.

"What about you, Stephen?" he said.

Stephen blushed, and wriggled, and stammered, and was understood to say that he'd be glad to help.

"Right," said Hal. "See Beth Wardrobe this afternoon. Have her fix you up with a costume."

A costume! Stephen looked ready to burst with pride.

There was a mild cough from beside Stephen. L. J. Hacker was volunteering to be the fourth messenger.

"OK," said Karl. "Back to the goddam set . . ."

"Why is it so easy to overlook Mr. Hacker?" said Emma, as they returned to work.

"I suppose it is because he is such a small, grey person," said Marco. "He is like a moth . . . or a mouse . . ."

"Both creatures that do a lot of damage out of all proportion to their size," said Hal.

One of the barns on the estate had been pressed into service as the Great Hall of the Prince, and here they filmed Brock looking superb in black velvet slashed with white, a pearl drop in one ear, a heavily jewelled hand resting upon a book, while an artist painted his portrait. At the end of the scene a servant dressed in black and white livery ran in with the news of Ariadne's supposed death, and Brock overturned book, and painting, and painter, and went storming down the length of the Great Hall with a pair of hounds yelping at his heels.

Another week, and shooting at the villa was completed. At the end of the last day, Emma sat at her desk in one of the courtyards. The trailers for Richard and Brock and Ariadne were parked in the shadow of the high wall. Brock was lounging beside her, waiting for a car to take him back to Lucca. Marco stood by the desk, checking the scene numbers for the next day's call sheet. Around them milled a bunch of extras, making their noisy, cheerful way towards a trestle table where the accountant gave them their daily pay. Emma glanced up and saw Walther making his way towards her through the crowd.

"Oh Lord," she said. "Here comes Walther. I suppose he's got another brilliant scene scribbled on one of those dreadful old bits of paper of his. If he's re-written the Minnehaha procession I shall scream . . ."

Walther, smiling, paused in front of Emma's desk.

"Great news, Emma," he said. "Ariadne has done me the honour of accepting my proposal."

Emma looked at him blankly.

"She's going to become Mrs. Walther Meister. I wanted you to be the first to know . . ."

It wasn't Emma that Walther was talking to.

It was Marco.

And before anyone could speak, Walther was gone.

The colour drained from Marco's face, leaving it grey. He closed his eyes, and for a moment Emma thought that he was going to faint. She put out her hand to him, but he brushed her aside, turned on his heel and walked away, gripping his script tightly to his chest. His left hand was clenched into a fist, and he was punching his thigh with every step he took, as though the physical pain would somehow alleviate his misery.

"The little bitch!" said Brock softly. "Mrs. Walther Meister . . . poor Leonidas!"

"Poor Marco," said Emma.

Brock swung round and looked at her.

"Sits the wind in that quarter?" he said.

"I think so," said Emma. "I think he's got it badly. That was a rotten trick of Walther's, to spring it on him suddenly like that."

"Poor boy," said Brock.

He sighed, and stood up.

"Well, he's not the first to believe that his girl is Juliet, and find out that she's Cressida. But you're right, Emma. It hurts. By God, it hurts . . ."

Brock left, and Emma started to mark up her script. The crowd of extras dwindled until the last of them had collected his pay and departed.

The accountant gathered together his papers and prepared to leave.

"Ciao, Emma!" he called, and hurried away.

Alone in the courtyard, Emma concentrated on her script. Tomorrow would be a busy day. They would return to La Rocca for the first time since the death of Leonidas, and they would shoot the last scene of the film: a string of riders, with a joyful Richard and Ariadne at their head, winding their way up the hill towards the fairy-tale castle where they would all live happily ever after.

Then they would move to the Wall of Death, now transformed into a monastery, and as soon as it was dark they would film the scenes of Brock and his men attacking the monastery and setting it on fire.

Gradually she became aware of angry voices. Two Italians were having a furious row. There was nothing uncommon about that, and she was about to block them out of her mind when she realized that the voices were coming from one of the trailers behind her. She swung round in alarm.

Richard's? No, that was locked up for the night. She breathed a sigh of relief.

Brock's? No, that was locked up also.

The voices were coming from the third trailer, and they belonged to Marco and Ariadne. They were shouting wildly at each other, their voices so harsh and rough with emotion that Emma hardly recognized them. Her knowledge of Italian was not good enough to cope with the flood of reproaches and vituperation, but suddenly she heard Marco cry out clearly, "Would you like me to tell Mr. Meister about Klara Sauss?"

There was a dead silence.

Thinking it was time they realized that they could be overheard, Emma started typing. The door of the trailer opened violently, and Marco came out, white-faced and angry. He checked as he saw Emma, and made an effort to return to his usual cool self.

"Women!" he said with a rueful grin. "Meaning Ariadne Andros!"

It was a brave try, but Emma could see that he was trembling.

"Ciao, Emma!" he said, and was gone.

13

The next day they left Lucca after lunch and drove to La Rocca. It was the first time they had been back there since the death of Leonidas, and everyone was very subdued. The shots of Ariadne, Richard and his followers riding up the hill were soon completed, and Ariadne and Richard were dismissed. Walther took Ariadne back to the villa, and Richard and Yorky returned to the farmhouse.

The stunt men changed costumes and became either Brock's henchmen or the monks they were attacking. The unit moved to the far end of the set, the Wall of Death.

There was nothing to remind anyone of the terrible afternoon when Leonidas had been killed. The battlements with the two hand-holds had disappeared altogether, and the main feature now was a square belfry. The cold grey stone wall had been repainted a cheerful terracotta. What had been the inner part of the castle was now a cloistered courtyard surrounded by the tiled roofs of the monastery buildings. There was an outer courtyard, and beyond, exactly where they had been before, the trailers for Richard, Brock and Ariadne, the stables, and the barn where the unit had their meals. The door of the nearby Props room was fitted with a big new padlock to prevent any more hoaxes with smoke-pots, and Emma noticed that the new Props man was careful to lock the door and keep the key in his pocket.

Karl rehearsed a couple of shots with Brock, and as soon as it was dark they began filming. First, a shot of Brock on his great black horse slashing down with his sword at a defenceless priest. Then a shot of Brock laughing triumphantly against a background of flames and thick black smoke. There was trouble with the smoke-pots for that shot. Karl was adamant that the smoke should writhe in heavy black coils behind Brock's head, but the smoke preferred to go straight up in the still night air and then disperse all over the place. By the time Karl had got the shot he wanted, the smoke-pots were almost empty. All the same, Emma saw that the new Props man was careful to put them away and lock the door on them.

They moved on to the next scene—a high shot of the belfry where a terrified young priest (Johnny, the fair-haired stunt man) was frantically sounding the tocsin.

A camera tower had been set up, and Karl, František and Emma joined the camera crew on the small platform. They were on a level with the top of the belfry, looking down over the tiled roofs of the monastery to the usual jumble of a film set. Tall towers supported the heavy lamps lighting the scene, each lamp with its attendant electrician. Beyond the filming area everything was very dark, and the ground looked black.

It was a tight squeeze on the camera platform. Emma crouched down, sitting on her heels, while the four men prepared the shot. Then Karl called Dave the stunt man to join him on the platform. Five people plus the camera was a tight squeeze, six people would be an impossibility. Emma climbed down again and Dave took her place.

But to do her job properly, a Continuity Girl needs to see the whole shot from the same viewpoint as the camera. Emma stood at the foot of the tower and looked up at the belfry. She couldn't even see the bell, let alone Johnny.

"*Signorina, venga qui!*"

A man was calling down to her from the top of a high tower set some way behind the camera tower. She thought at first that it was one of the lighting towers, and then she noticed that the wooden stages were packed with mattresses and cardboard fall-boxes under a covering of straw matting. It was going to be used by the stunt men later in the attack.

The man called again.

"Venga qui!"

Emma tucked her script under her arm and started to climb the ladder. It was a long way to the top, and the ladder flexed and bounced as she went up, but it was not nearly so frightening as the climb to the battlements had been, because now the ground was out of sight in the darkness. She reached the top, and the man helped her on to the wooden platform.

At a signal from František, all the lights came on, and the belfry stood out brilliantly in the midst of the surrounding blackness. Emma hugged herself. She had an excellent view.

They rehearsed the scene, and then Karl called for a take. High in the belfry the young priest tolled the bell until a bolt hit him in the breast and sent him tumbling down into the darkness, where fall-boxes and mattresses were waiting to break his fall.

By the third take, Karl was satisfied.

"OK, Hal," he called. "Let's break for supper."

"Supper-break, one hour!" called Hal.

"Pausa—un' ora!" called Marco.

The lights went out immediately, and the set was left in absolute blackness. The unit cursed. Startled, Emma dropped her script on to the wooden platform of her tower. She knelt down, felt for it in the darkness, picked it up, and was surprised to find that she was alone. The man who helped her up must have hurried down the ladder as soon as Hal called the supper-break. She'd have to climb down on her own. Still kneeling, she felt along the edge of the platform and groped for the top of the ladder. It wasn't there. Puzzled, she ran her hand carefully along the edge of the platform. At the corner she shifted her position and ran her hand along the next edge. No ladder. She tried the third edge, and the fourth. She had felt carefully along each edge of the platform, and there was no ladder. A slight feeling of panic gripped her, but she fought it down. She'd just have to stay there for an hour until the rest of the crew got back. She could see them moving under the lights in the courtyard, streaming towards the lighted barn. She could see the new Props man dutifully locking up the Props room before he too went off for his supper. There were lights on in two of the trailers. She wasn't surprised to see a light in Brock's, but she was surprised to see a light in Richard's. Surely Richard and Yorky left the set hours ago, as soon as Karl finished shooting with them.

A thrill of fear shot through her. Could Richard and Yorky be somewhere on the set—perhaps down below her in the dark?

She thought she heard somebody moving about, and called out, but there was no answer.

Only a slight sound of crackling, and a faint smell of smoke.

The straw matting down below was on fire.

In the barn everyone queued for supper, laughed, joked, ate and drank. Nobody missed Emma except Stephen, and he wasn't worried. Richard and Yorky joined Karl at his table, and they talked for a few minutes.

"Hal!" called Karl. "Where's Emma? Tell her I want her!"

Hal glanced around.

"I'll have a look for her," he said.

He lifted the straw matting that hung down the side of the barn and looked out into the courtyard to see if Emma was there. The courtyard was deserted, but his eye was caught by a glow of light at the far side of the Wall of Death. A flickering glow of light. Fire!

He forgot about Emma. Fire was priority number one, and this looked like a fire on the camera tower. Quickly and quietly he collected the camera crew, the stunt men, Marco and Stephen. They ran across the empty courtyard, swung round the corner of the monastery wall, and saw that the assault tower was on fire.

"At least it's not the camera tower," said Hal. "But it's damned close to it!"

"Help!" screamed Emma. "Help!"

The men on the ground were shocked into sudden immobility. For the first time they realized that there was somebody on the tower.

"My God! It's Emma!" shouted Hal. "Get the safety gear— FAST!"

The camera crew ran off to the Props room.

"Fall-boxes from the belfry!" shouted Hal.

The stunt men ran to the belfry and began dragging fall-boxes and mattresses.

The smoke was curling up round Emma, blinding and choking her. Flames were spurting out from below. The straw matting had set the cardboard fall-boxes ablaze, and now the fire was catching hold of the mattresses. The wooden platform was getting unbearably hot. Once the platform collapsed, it would take her down with it into the roaring furnace below.

A man came running. Bob, the camera operator.

"Marco, quick!" he shouted. "That damned Props man has locked up all the safety gear! Come and make him get it out!"

Marco ran off with him.

Johnny, the stunt man, still wearing his costume as the young priest, was organizing the setting up of a ring of fall-boxes and mattresses round the base of the tower.

Hal looked up at the blazing tower.

"She'll never jump," he said despairingly. "She'll never jump . . ."

Stephen, helping to stack the fall-boxes, suddenly remembered Emma saying, "If Hal told me to jump, I'd do it . . ."

He tried to pull Hal's arm, and Hal, unseeing, shook him off. Stephen grabbed at Hal and pulled him round to face him.

"Tell her to jump, Hal!" he shouted. "She'll d-do it if she c-can hear your voice. If only she c-can hear you above all this racket . . ."

Hal gripped Stephen's arm and stared at him hard.

Stephen shouted, "It *is* safe for her to j-jump, isn't it?"

"Safer than staying up there!" shouted Johnny. "She might hurt herself on the fall-boxes, but it's her only chance!"

"Quiet!" roared Hal. "Quiet!"

The babble of voices died down, but the crackle and roar of the flames was as furious as ever. Could Emma possibly hear his voice?

Hal stood back, threw back his head and shouted, "Emma! Jump! Emma! Jump!"

Johnny and others took up the cry.

"Jump! Emma! Jump! Emma!" they shouted.

"No! No!" shouted Stephen. "Emma will only j-jump if she c-can hear *Hal's* voice!"

His unaccustomed air of authority impressed them, and they kept quiet and left the calling to Hal.

He called again and again, his great voice battling with the noise of the fire, but there was no response.

High on the blazing tower, deafened by the roar of the flames, coughing and half-blinded with the smoke, Emma was on her knees, trying desperately to beat back the flames with her heavy script.

"Emma! Jump! Emma! Jump!"

Hal's voice.

She crawled to the edge of the platform, but the flames leaped up at her and she could see nothing beyond them.

"Emma! Jump! Emma! Jump!"

She couldn't jump. Her legs were weak and trembling, she was exhausted, she had no strength left. And she was afraid.

"Emma! Jump!"

Hal was down there, waiting for her.

She couldn't jump. But she could—she could let herself fall over the edge . . . Still on her knees, holding the script before her face to shield her from the searing heat, she leaned forward and toppled over, falling through the flames which snatched at her hair, her clothes.

A cry went up from the men watching below.

Her body hit something hard. The ground? But the ground seemed to be crumpling under her. Or was it her own body crumpling amid all the roaring?

She had landed on a pile of mattresses and fall-boxes. Hal and Johnny ran to her and pulled the boxes away from the blazing tower into the darkness. Johnny beat out the flames burning her clothes, and Hal wrapped his sweater round her. She still had her script tightly clenched in both hands, and Johnny had to prise her fingers open to release it.

Emma opened her eyes.

A young priest was holding her hands. Behind him the blazing tower crackled and roared and flared. A priest? Then she must be dying. His face was familiar, but she couldn't quite remember where she'd seen him before. The air was hot and full of flying sparks, but she felt as cold as ice. Other faces leaned over her, sweating, scorched and streaked with black. She searched frantically in the flickering light for the only face that mattered.

Hal.

It was the last thing she saw before she fainted.

Marco and the others came running with fire-extinguishers and asbestos blankets. By now the word had spread, and most of the men came with them—stage-hands, grips, electricians, painters and carpenters. Gradually they brought the flames under control, and at last the fire was out. The tower was a sodden mass of ash and burned mattresses, and a bitter smell hung in the air. The work of clearing up began. Stephen picked up Emma's script. The heavy cover had protected much of it, but the pages were still smouldering with little sparks catching the night breeze and eating along the edge of the paper.

He saw a hunched figure sitting in the darkness at the foot of the belfry. It was Marco, his face in his hands, sobbing like a tired child. Stephen sat down beside him and touched his shoulder with awkward shyness.

"She's going to b-be all right, M-Marco," he said. "H-Hal says she'll be all right . . ."

He wasn't sure that Marco could hear him.

"L-look," said Stephen. "I've g-got Emma's script. She's g-going to want that. Would you help me to t-tidy it up for her?"

Marco stared at him in a daze.

"It's something to d-do," said Stephen helplessly.

Marco made an effort. Together they turned the pages of the script, pouncing on the little sparks, smothering them, smoothing the coloured pages covered in Emma's notes, rubbing away the tindery edges. They went on turning the pages for a long time, long after all the sparks had gone out. In the distance they could hear the sounds of the unit wrapping up and pulling out, voices calling, doors slamming, cars starting and driving away.

Next morning Emma lay in her bed in her hotel room and wished she were dead. Her body was unbroken, but she was bruised and scorched, her hands were bandaged and her hair had been burned. She tried to trim the worst bits with a pair of nail scissors, but she was too tired, and burst into tears when she saw the result. Stripes of sunlight entered the room through the venetian blinds. She looked at them dully and fell asleep. When she awoke, the stripes had disappeared.

Slowly she became aware that somebody was tapping on her door. Let them tap. She couldn't be bothered to tell them to go away. The door opened slightly, and Stephen's beaky owlet face appeared.

"Oh, g-good," he said. "You're awake."

He came into the room carrying an extravagant bouquet of pink and white roses tied with streamers of matching ribbon. He left the door open, and before Emma could gather sufficient strength to tell him to shut it, Hal arrived. He came straight over to Emma, took her bandaged hands in his, and stood looking down at her.

Emma didn't know whether to cry or laugh. Hal holding her hands, Stephen clutching his bouquet with the ridiculous ribbons.

"For goodness sake, Hal," she said, "find a chair and sit down. And you too, Stephen."

"Bossy as ever," said Hal, as they sat down. "You must be feeling better. Now, Emma, what in God's name were you doing on the tower?"

"There wasn't room for me on the camera platform," said Emma. "One of the men helped me up."

"Who was it?" asked Hal.

"I don't know. I suppose he was one of the stage-hands. Anyhow, when the lights went out he had disappeared, and so had the ladder."

"Having a crafty smoke," said Hal. "Tossed it away still alight. Went off to supper. And the straw caught fire."

"It looks like a d-deliberate attempt at m-murder," said Stephen indignantly. "But who could p-possibly want to k-kill Emma?"

"Nobody loves a Continuity Girl," said Emma wryly.

She looked up at Hal and her heart turned over.

"Hal," she said, "could it have been Richard—or Yorky? I thought I saw a light in Richard's trailer at supper-time—but surely they left the set long before it got dark?"

Hal let go of Emma's hands.

"Yes, they went home," he said, "but Karl asked Richard to come back and see him at supper-time. Can you remember— when did the fire start?"

"I could see everybody going towards the barn for supper," she said. "I think that was when the fire started."

"Then Richard and Yorky are in the clear," said Hal. They were talking to Karl then. He wanted you. I went to look for you, and saw the fire. So it was thanks to Richard and Yorky that we got to you in time."

"Thank God you did!" said Emma, and shivered. "I suppose it could have been an accident. The man *might* have climbed down the ladder, and somebody *could* have moved it, not knowing I was up there. The fire *might* have been started by a cigarette end—"

"It sounds far more likely than Richard and Yorky trying to kill you," said Hal. "Why should they? Be reasonable, Emma."

She closed her eyes. She was desperately tired, she ached all over, and her hair was a mess. She had nearly died on the blazing tower. And Hal was telling her that it was an accident. Hal was telling her to be reasonable! She took a deep breath. She would get a grip on herself. She would be professional. She would be—reasonable.

"What time is it?" she asked, and was annoyed to hear that her voice was quavery.

"About n-nine o'clock," said Stephen.

"In the evening?" asked Emma, astonished. Her voice was now perfectly steady. "What time do we leave for Siena tomorrow?"

"*We* leave at eight A.M.," said Hal. "But *you* stay here. The company doctor says you're to have a complete rest, and the Palio is no place for an invalid."

"I shan't be a liability, if that's what you mean," said Emma, flaring up. "And I'm not missing the Palio! I'll probably never have another chance to see it as long as I live."

The stereotyped phrase reminded them all that the previous night Emma's expectation of life had been terrifyingly short. There was an awkward silence.

Stephen suddenly noticed that he was still holding the bouquet of roses.

"I—er—I've b-brought these for you," he said, and thrust the flowers into her arms.

"Oh, thank you, Stephen," said Emma. "They're lovely. It's very—very sweet of you . . ."

She buried her face in the pink and white roses, and the ribbons spilled over the bed. She had a lump in her throat, and tears in her eyes, because of all the people on the picture, Stephen was the one least able to afford the expensive luxury of flowers.

After Hal and Stephen had gone, Emma lay in bed and tried to take herself in hand.

You've got to face up to it, Emma, she told herself firmly. Hal only came to see you as a matter of duty. He would visit any member of the crew who was off sick. He's not interested in you as a woman, and there's nothing you can do about it.

It didn't help.

That night she sobbed her heart out, and only fell asleep when she was utterly exhausted.

She must be dreaming. She was flying over the Piazza San Marco with a flock of pigeons. Down below she could see the Basilica with a wedding group posing for photographs. The bride was Stella Camay in a white silk pants suit. The photographer had an old-fashioned plate camera on a wooden tripod, and his head was hidden in a drape of black velvet. Click! He had taken his picture.

But now the bride was Ariadne, wearing her white swansdown cloak and carrying a bouquet of pink and white roses. She was smiling up at her bridegroom, Leonidas. And then suddenly he wasn't Leonidas at all, but Walther, and he was scattering crumbs over the pavement for the pigeons. But the crumbs were poisoned, and as Emma flew down towards them she could hear herself crying to Walther, "Go away! Go away! Can't you see that I'm a bell-tower?" And she awoke with a vivid picture of a young priest desperately pulling on a bell-rope, and the sound of a distant clock striking seven.

Emma jumped out of bed, ran to the window and pulled up the blind. It was seven o'clock on a fine sunny morning, July

2nd, the day of the Palio. And thanks to a dream she knew who had been responsible for the deaths of Stella and Leonidas, and why he had done it.

Walther Meister.

Walther Meister, in love with Ariadne.

He had killed Stella Camay so that Ariadne could take her place.

He had killed Leonidas so that Walther could take *his* place.

And he had got away with it.

"An accident!" he had said, after he fired the bolt that killed Leonidas. And everybody believed him.

Walther Meister, the man who could get away with murder.

14

The Campo in Siena looked very different from the last time Emma had seen it. The Torre Mangia still soared serene and lovely, the most beautiful bell-tower in the world, but the square itself had been transformed into a colossal amphitheatre. Flags flew from the rooftops and balconies, and scarlet hangings decorated all the windows overlooking the Campo. In front of the ancient buildings tiers of wooden benches rose behind padded crash barriers, and in front of the crash barriers there was a broad ribbon of yellow earth which ran all round the Campo as the combined parade-ground and race-course for the Palio. Inside the ring of earth was the centre of the Campo where ten thousand people would stand, crammed together like herrings in a barrel, prevented from spilling on to the track by a broad barrier, waist-high, just right for little girls to sit on and little boys to jump off. People were milling about, even though the parade would not start for several hours, and the atmosphere was crackling with electricity like a cat's fur.

The camera crews took up their positions inside the central barrier, and the crowds built up round them until the cameras were black islands in a multi-coloured sea, and the crews could hardly move. Soon there were officials in black and white mediaeval costume moving about on the track, and Karl's costumed messengers—Hal, Marco, Stephen and L. J. Hacker —merged with them. The buzz of conversation sounded like an immense beehive. "One hundred thousand people watch the race, and ten thousand of them are standing in the centre." Emma could well believe it.

Suddenly Hacker came hurrying along in his harlequin costume and spoke urgently to Karl.

"Message from Walther," he said. "He's having some language difficulty with his Italian cameraman. Can he have Emma to stand by and translate for him?"

Emma felt once more the familiar stab of fear, and despite the heat of the day she felt cold. But what possible reason could she give Karl for refusing Walther's request? "I suspect your cousin Walther is a murderer, and I want to keep as far away from him as I possibly can?" Then common sense stepped in. Walther had no idea she suspected him. Why should he want to harm her? She must be reasonable . . .

Karl jerked his head at her impatiently, and she started to make her way through the tightly packed crowd.

"Permesso! Permesso!" Her experience of forcing her way through crowded Roman buses stood her in good stead. She shoved her way unceremoniously forward, using her script as a battering-ram. The heavy binder was scuffed and scorched from the fire, but it was still very solid, and at the top was a large and vicious bulldog clip. She had on occasions brought this weapon crashing down upon the questing hand of an over-familiar young—or not so young—man. Walther was unlikely to be amorous, but if he came too close she would defend herself with the script.

She wished now that she had shared her suspicions of Walther with somebody trustworthy—Hal, perhaps, or Marco. But Hal had seemed more than usually preoccupied when they were in the car together, and whenever she had seen Marco he had seemed very busy. Well, Marco was the link between the film unit and the authorities of the Palio, so of course he had been busy. He looked quite handsome in his black and white harlequin tunic and striped hose, and wore his costume as though he had been born to it. Hal had looked a little self-conscious in his harlequin tunic at first, but now he carried himself easily. Emma smiled to herself as Stephen and Hacker went along the track in their costumes—a pair of spindle-shanked magpies who would never look at home in their borrowed feathers. Even so, they were less conspicuous than the handful of officials who were wearing modern clothes.

Forcing her way to the Torre Mangia, Emma reached Walther's camera. The cameraman—one of the extra crews who had arrived the previous day—was a man she had worked with before on another picture.

"*Ciao,* Giancarlo!" she said.

"*Ciao,* Emma!" he said, and his face lit up. Clearly he had been having trouble with Walther, and regarded Emma as an ally.

She took up her position on the right of the camera. Walther was on the left, and beside him stood the company doctor. Emma was surprised to see him there, but she found his presence very reassuring. If Walther had any thought of harming her, he wouldn't want an expert witness at his elbow. Surely common sense was right, and Walther simply wanted her to translate his remarks to Giancarlo. Knowing Giancarlo, she wondered how Walther would react if she translated some of the camera operator's remarks in return . . .

The camera was jammed up against the waist-high barrier, pointing directly at the chapel at the foot of the Torre Mangia. Beside it was the big wooden door with the little door beside it, like a cat-flap. She could see the iron grille in the wall, the grille with the clover-leaf in the middle. A single pigeon was perched on the clover-leaf. Emma wondered where all its fellows had gone, and why it had not gone with them.

The excitement was building up, and the noise was deafening. Emma could no longer even pretend to hear what Walther was shouting at her across the camera. He beckoned her to stand beside him. She spoke quickly to Giancarlo.

"Signor Meister wants me to stand beside him," she said. "Please, Giancarlo, if I need help, can I count on you? I am a little afraid of him."

"The old goat!" said Giancarlo, misunderstanding the reason for her anxiety. "OK, I'll keep my eye on him, Emma. But I bet you'll be a match for him. I've still got a scar on my arm from that damned script of yours . . ."

Emma squeezed round the camera and stood between Giancarlo and Walther. She had an uneasy feeling that Giancarlo was enjoying the situation. The crowd pressed tightly against them.

It was nearly five o'clock. Officials began clearing stragglers off the track while police and First Aid men took up their positions. Emma saw Hacker and Stephen hurrying by to their respective posts and shouted at them to take off their sunglasses. Guiltily, they did so. If they happened to be seen in the film, they might just pass as members of the mediaeval crowd.

"Look, there's Marco!" said Giancarlo. "*Ciao*, Marco!"

Marco came towards them.

"*Ciao*, Giancarlo!" he said. "But—what are you doing here, Emma? I thought you were with Karl's unit?"

"Karl sent me over to look after Walther," said Emma. She made a little grimace and Giancarlo laughed.

"She's afraid the old goat is going to try something on," he said. "But I've told her I'll look after her!"

Giancarlo clearly regarded his unaccustomed role of protector as highly comical, but Marco did not smile, and Emma reflected that he was unlikely to be amused by anything to do with Walther.

"You do that!" he said, in such a way that Giancarlo stopped laughing. "Emma's a good friend of mine. *Ciao*, Emma!"

He moved away down the track to take up his position near the Palazzo Pubblico.

Emma looked around. Every window overlooking the Campo was crammed with spectators, and even the rooftops had been pressed into service as grand-stands. Every seat on the crowded benches had been filled long ago, and every inch of space in the central area was filled with sweating and excited humanity. Here and there she could see clusters of coloured balloons bobbing above the heads of the crowd. The sun was still blazing out of a cloudless sky, but the shadows of the tall buildings had crept over the Campo, and now only the upper parts of the buildings were in sunlight. Soon even that would disappear. It was five o'clock on a warm summer evening, and Siena was waiting.

DONG!

    DONG!

        DONG!

            DONG!

                DONG!

Five strokes of Sunto, the great bell of the Torre Mangia. Crack!

A fire-cracker signalled the start of the parade, and mounted carabinieri in black and gold came galloping into the Campo, casting long shadows across the yellow earth. The parade followed in an uproar of cheering and clapping, of drums rolling and church bells ringing. Emma could see nothing over the mass of people, and she suddenly felt a twinge of misgiving. Would the parade be as full of production value as Marco had indicated, or would it consist of a lot of elderly gentlemen walking slowly and out of step, like a procession of English academics? The crowd was cheering and waving, and still she could see nothing. Then the parade swung round the San Martino corner and came towards her.

Living playing-cards in red and black were marching over the yellow track, escorting a rider in scarlet who carried the great black and white banner of Siena. Behind him came musicians playing long silver trumpets. Then more playing-card people, carrying a whole forest of banners in scarlet and blue and gold. They passed so close to her that she could have leaned over the barrier and touched them.

She was ashamed to have doubted Marco. Production value? The parade was solid, 22-carat production value. She wondered how much Karl was paying for the privilege of filming it. Or rather, how little.

Giancarlo began filming, concentrating on the scarlet rider. Then the silver trumpets. Then the forest of banners. Then he cut the camera, and let the rest of the parade go past. He was waiting for the standard-bearers.

"Watch this!" he muttered to Emma as the first pair of standard-bearers came towards them. They were tall young men, each carrying a flag with a green and gold heraldic device. The procession stopped at the San Martino corner. Giancarlo started the camera. A roll on the drums, and the two young men tossed the heavy flags high in the air and caught them again. They held the flags high and whirled them in dazzling patterns against the sky, as precise and as beautiful as a display of formation flying. For nearly two hours the procession went by, each part of the city with its special costumes and banners and its standard-bearers leaping over each other, sweeping the heavy flags close above the ground, always in perfect time with the beating of the drums. Emma glanced back across the Campo—a dark mass of cheering spectators in the centre, coloured balloons still bobbing about above them, the brilliant parade filling the yellow ribbon of the race-track, and high in the air the coloured flags rising and falling, like tropical butterflies dancing in the evening sunlight.

The last of the standard-bearers passed in front of Giancarlo; he cut the camera and waited. "*Carroccio,*" he said to Emma. She wondered what the *carroccio* would look like. The crowd had been cheering with noisy enthusiasm for nearly two hours. Now the cheering had changed to a deep-throated roar. As usual, Emma had to wait until the procession turned the San Martino corner, but then she had a perfect view. Four white oxen were drawing a heavy, box-shaped cart, its high wooden sides brightly painted, its wooden wheels heavily gilded. Six musicians stood on board, sounding silver trumpets. And in the middle of the *carroccio*, like a great sail on a slowly moving ship, was the Palio itself, a silk banner bearing a painted image of the Virgin Mary. This was the very heart of the festival.

Giancarlo panned with it as the procession slowly moved towards the Palazzo Pubblico. Then he cut the camera, and once more he waited. The people from the parade were stepping up on to the benches in front of the Palazzo. Many of them moved in a slow and stately fashion like the *carroccio* and its white oxen, now lumbering out of sight. Karl took the opportunity to send Stephen along the track to Walther.

"Mr. M-Meister," he said, "would you p-please film the clock on the t-tower when it strikes seven?"

Emma passed the message to Giancarlo, who nodded and lined up the shot.

"Emma, these c-costumes are great!" said Stephen. "M-Marco told me to say, '*P-Permesso,*' and then g-go straight wherever I have to go, and he's quite right, it works p-perfectly. My w-word, I'm going to m-miss all this t-tomorrow!"

He turned and ran back along the track towards the starting-post. Emma thought she could see Hal moving towards the Palazzo Pubblico, but she couldn't be sure. There were so many black and white harlequin costumes moving about there.

The horses were led out by their riders, and the crowd cheered them. Giancarlo switched on the camera, and Emma could feel the faint vibration and hear the soft, steady whirr of the moving film. A hush spread over the crowd. They might have been a hundred thousand statues as they waited for Sunto to announce that it was seven o'clock, and time for the race to begin. Siena was holding its breath.

A sudden clatter of wings startled Emma. She turned her head sharply and saw that the pigeon had flown up from the clover-leaf. Only Emma noticed it, and only Emma saw the reason for its flight. To the right of the clover-leaf, a gun pointing through the grille.

Pointing at her.

DONG! The first stroke of the bell.

So the blazing tower at La Rocca had not been an accident.

It had been a deliberate attempt at murder.

And this was another.

Jammed up against the barrier by the pressure of the crowd, Emma was a perfect target.

DONG! The second stroke.

The gunman, invisible in the darkness behind the grille, must be a hired killer.

No need to ask who had hired him.

The man who had seen to it that she would be in the appointed place of execution at the appointed hour.

Walther Meister.

DONG! The third stroke.

Rage swept over her, a cold fury that Walther should have got away with it so often, and that he was going to get away with it again.

DONG! The fourth stroke.

Stephen was right: no film was worth the sacrifice of a single human life.

But that includes *mine,* she thought.

Wake up, Emma! Think! Think!

DONG! The fifth stroke.

The padded barrier protected her from the waist down. She could duck down behind it. But then the gunman might kill somebody in the crowd, and he could still lie in wait for her later on.

Her only defence was the inch-thick script of *The Trumpets of Tuscany* in its heavy cover. She raised it to her breast and faced her unseen enemy.

DONG! The sixth stroke.

I've been a foolish and ignorant woman, she thought, and I've wasted a lot of my life. But I've seen the Torre Mangia by moonlight, and I've seen the parade of the Palio. At least I'm going out on a high note. All right, you bastard, I'm ready for you!

> DONG! The last stroke.
>
> A spurt of flame.

Crack!

The signal for the start of the race was the signal for the gunman to fire.

The immense crowd erupted as the horses surged forward. Walther lurched against her, and she pushed him away impatiently, no longer afraid of him.

And then realized that she was still alive.

The gunman had fired, and she was still alive!

Shaking, she looked at her script.

It was unmarked.

She looked towards the grille.

The gun was no longer there.

Walther leaned against her once more, and once more she pushed him away, and found that her hand was covered in blood.

The company doctor, standing on the other side of Walther, was sweating and shouting with the crowd, and had noticed nothing. Emma grabbed his collar with her bloodstained hand and, as he turned angrily, she thrust Walther towards him. The expression on the doctor's face changed swiftly from anger to bewilderment and then to shock, and Emma knew that Walther was dead.

The gunman's bullet had found the wrong target.

She laughed.

She had once thought that if Walther tried to commit murder he would kill the wrong person. With a beautiful irony, his hired gunman had done exactly that.

But what had happened to the gunman?

The gun had disappeared from the grille, so presumably the man had disappeared too. On the opposite side of the track there was a sudden flurry of movement as two carabinieri ran through the cat-flap into the darkness beyond.

The doctor was shouting for help, but his voice was drowned in the general uproar as a hundred thousand enthusiasts urged on the riders and the horses.

The horses!

Any second now they would come racing past.

Emma glanced at Giancarlo. With his eye to the viewfinder he had concentrated on filming the clock, and hadn't noticed the gunman. He didn't even know that Walther was dead. So much for Giancarlo as a protector!

Emma put her hand lightly on his shoulder.

"Here they come!" she said.

Giancarlo swung the camera into position and filmed the horses as they came thundering round the San Martino corner. He grinned at Emma and gave the thumbs-up sign.

"Ben Hur!" he said happily.

Emma strained her eyes to watch the horses. They passed the Palazzo Pubblico and turned right to run up the hill. Judging from the way the heads in the crowd were turning, the horses had passed Karl's camera and were on their second lap. The horses themselves were hidden by the crowd, but she could just see the jockeys' arms flailing as they slashed at each other with the heavy ox-hide whips.

"OK, Giancarlo," she said. "Here they come again."

As they entered the San Martino corner with its dangerous downward slope, two of the horses crashed and fell. The jockeys rolled over, and the horses scrambled up and ran on, riderless. First Aid men in modern dress ran forward and pulled the jockeys to safety.

Giancarlo swore at the rescuers.

"Cretins! Assassins!" he howled. "You've ruined my picture!"

At that moment, the great bell of the Torre Mangia spoke softly.

Emma looked up.

High on the sunlit bell-tower stood a figure in a harlequin tunic of black and white.

She stared in utter disbelief, and then some instinct told her to get a picture of him.

She grabbed Giancarlo.

"*Su, su, Giancarlo—la Torre!*" she gasped, and Giancarlo, after one startled look at her face, tilted the camera up and up, searching through the viewfinder for the top of the tower.

He found it.

"*Gesù Maria!*" he muttered.

In that one terrible moment, Emma knew the truth about death and *The Trumpets of Tuscany*.

It was the harlequin who had killed Stella, and Leonidas.

Now he had killed Walther, and not by mistake.

Emma had been wrong, wrong, wrong all the time.

As the harlequin moved, she heard a whisper from the great bell echoing her thoughts—WRONG . . . WRONG . . . WRONG . . .

Beside her, Giancarlo suddenly tilted the camera down to the ground, and then up again to the bell-tower, and Emma realized that he was rehearsing the camera movement, in case the harlequin should fall.

Two carabinieri had reached the top of the tower, and could just be seen as shadowy figures in the background.

The harlequin turned and looked at them.

Emma stiffened.

Quite deliberately, the harlequin climbed out on to the white balustrade and stood poised for a moment. He raised one hand in a final gesture—was it defiance or farewell?

Then he fell headlong.

Giancarlo's camera swooped down with him, down and down and down, until the black and white figure crashed to the ground and was mercifully hidden from view by the horses streaking past in a blur of colour.

The Palio was over, and Emma's world had fallen apart.

15

"The Palio is the only survivor of the many cruel and violent games which took place in Siena during the Middle Ages. It takes its name from the silken pallium, or banner, the prize for which the contestants battle so fiercely. This banner bears the image of the Blessed Virgin, and the festival is held in her honour. The official institution of the Palio is recorded in a document of 1310, but it is known that the custom began at a much earlier date . . ."

That is what the guide-books tell you.

But the old people say that the Palio derives from a pre-Christian festival held in honour of an older, grimmer Mother. Her worship demanded human sacrifice, and her festival culminated in a fight to the death and the pouring of a man's blood upon the thirsty earth.

Certainly some of the old women of Siena whispered together in secret, and smiled knowingly as they thought of the two victims who had been sacrificed at the Old One's festival: one man murdered, and one man leaping from the tower to a terrible death.

Blood had been spilled upon the earth.

The Old One would be satisfied.

16

A few nights after the Palio, Karl and the crew gathered in one of Lucca's cinemas to see the results of their filming, rushed from the laboratories in Rome.

Karl sat there in silence, and alone. The seat on his left, where Walther always sat, was empty.

In the next row there was another empty seat, and Emma's heart ached when she looked at it.

Nobody spoke as shot after shot appeared on the screen—the long mediaeval parade, the start of the race, and the finish.

Occasionally the screen showed glimpses of Hal and his messengers—Marco, Stephen and Hacker—wearing their black and white harlequin costumes. In the ordinary way this would have prompted ribald shrieks and catcalls, but today there was silence. There was only the sound of the projector, and of the projectionist himself moving about.

The harsh white beam of light cut through the heavy darkness, and blue cigarette smoke drifted upwards as the pictures continued.

Karl watched it all in bitter silence.

At last he cried out furiously, "A man jumps off a high tower in full view of thousands of people, and not one of you had the goddam sense to get a picture of it?"

Then Giancarlo's film appeared on the screen, and Emma sat very still. She and Giancarlo were the only people who knew what they were about to see, and she was not sure that even Giancarlo had quite realized what he was filming. A camera operator, watching a scene through a small viewfinder, concentrates on composing his picture, and the actors who appear in it are mere figures in a landscape. Seeing the final pictures enlarged on the cinema screen might give Giancarlo a nasty jolt.

The film began. First the scarlet rider with the black and white flag at the head of the procession. Then the silver trumpets. Then the forest of banners. The manoeuvres with the flags. The Carroccio with the Palio lumbering towards the camera, passing and moving away. The clock on the tower, signalling the start of the race.

Seven o'clock.

The first sweep of the horses round the San Martino corner, the riders flogging each other with their whips, Giancarlo's "Ben Hur" shot. There was a low murmur of approval.

Then came the second sweep round the corner, when the two horses fell and lost their riders, a shot that was ruined as the officials in modern dress came running into the picture to pull the jockeys to the side of the track.

Then suddenly the camera tilted sharply upwards, up and up to the top of the Torre Mangia. The watchers in the cinema drew in their breath, shocked, and held it.

The focus sharpened.

There was the harlequin figure on the sunlit parapet. He turned and looked back into the darkness of the tower behind him. Then he climbed out on to the stone balustrade, looked down for a moment, raised his arm in a final salute, and fell headlong, the camera tilting down with him. Then the horses thundered past and the picture blurred and stopped.

There was a stunned silence in the darkened cinema.

Giancarlo rushed out into the corridor and was violently sick. The door thudded softly close behind him, shutting out the retching sound.

The lights came up.

Still nobody spoke.

They didn't even look at each other.

At last Karl cleared his throat and said quietly, "That shot, Emma. I'm going to use it for Brock's death."

"But, Karl—" she said.

"I know we planned to end the film with a fight between Brock and Richard on the steps," said Karl. "I'm going to scrub that. Brock and Richard will slug it out on top of the tower, and then Brock will fall. Have the Art Department make us a matching tower-top at La Rocca."

He swung round to face the shocked and silent unit.

"I'm going to use that shot as a tribute to my cousin Walther," said Karl. "He must have known that he was dying, but he hung on, and he directed the finest shot in the whole goddam picture."

He turned suddenly to Stephen.

"You," he said. "When you write that goddam book of yours, you make sure you put that in—a tribute to my cousin, Walther Meister!"

"Yes, Mr. M-Meister," whispered Stephen. His face was white.

Karl turned and put out his arm in the old affectionate gesture towards his cousin. He saw the empty chair, and Emma, catching the script as it dropped from his hand, thought that this was the moment when he first realized that Walther was indeed dead. Karl's face shrivelled, his body drooped, and he became, quite suddenly, an old man. He walked mechanically towards the door, somebody opened it for him and he went out.

There was a brief pause, and then the rest of the unit filed out silently.

Only Emma remained, pretending to make notes in her script until they had all gone, and she was alone. Her throat felt tight, and her eyes were brimming over with tears. Nobody would ever know that Walther was dead before the harlequin had appeared on the tower, and that Emma was responsible for getting "the finest shot in the goddam picture." If the shot was remembered at all, it would be as a symbol of the dying Walther's heroic devotion to duty. And when she thought of the picture of the harlequin on the tower, and the harlequin falling, she half hoped that she might come in time to believe in the story of the heroic Walther. For the harlequin had been her comrade; they had worked and argued and laughed together. And Emma wept for the Marco she had known.

"How art thou fallen from Heaven, O Lucifer, son of the morning! . . ."

17

After Marco's death, nothing would ever be quite the same again.

Hacker, that writer of minor domestic comedies, drank several cognacs, snarled at his wife, locked himself in the toilet and emerged three hours later with a speech for Brock to deliver at the end of the film. It owed something to Bogart's renunciation speech in *Casablanca,* but it lifted *The Trumpets of Tuscany* on to a new and higher plane.

When his death-scene on the bell-tower was filmed, Brock whispered the words with passionate intensity, a man bidding farewell to life. He seemed to be watching the Palio taking place in the Campo far below him, and when he finished speaking he raised his hand in salute as Marco had done, and fell headlong from the tower. Brock's tower was only ten feet above the ground, surrounded by fall-boxes and mattresses, but in the finished film he and Marco would be indistinguishable.

As she listened to Brock, Emma recalled Marco sitting at the café in the Campo and saying, "I do not belong to Siena, but when I watch the Palio being run, oh, how I shall wish that I did!" She pushed the memory away. It hurt too much.

A few weeks later, shooting was completed, and the unit left La Rocca, which reverted to its previous peaceful existence as a gently crumbling ruin.

Karl Meister flew home to California and his wife Minna.

The script writer and the actors departed.

So did Beth Wardrobe, Babs Hairdresser and Charles Make-Up.

Camera crew, sound crew, electricians, stage-hands and construction crews, they all packed up their gear and returned to their respective homes.

Emma went back to her apartment in Rome, and there one evening, a week later, she had a gathering of those members of the unit who were taking a holiday in Rome before going back to England.

Hal was there, and Stephen, and Penny the Production Secretary, plus several of the stunt men, including Dave and Johnny. They sat around on the roof-garden, where orange-trees grew in tubs and cascades of jasmine frothed over a white-painted trellis. All the domes and rooftops of Rome lay spread out before them, glowing in the warmth of the summer evening. Emma circulated with a tray of glasses clinking with ice. Inevitably everybody talked about *The Trumpets of Tuscany*, and just as inevitably they talked about Marco.

"B-but why?" asked Stephen. "Why did he d-do such terrible things?"

"I think," said Emma slowly, "that it was fear. Fear drives people to do the most terrible things. What Marco wanted desperately was security. You see, he came from a very old, very wealthy family which lost everything during the war."

"I d-didn't know that," said Stephen.

"I did," said Emma. "But it's only since I came back here to Rome that I've had time to think what that really meant. Just imagine—all his life, Italy had been Germany's ally. Then suddenly Mussolini fell, Italy declared war on Germany, and the Nazis occupied Rome. Then after another year of war, the Americans entered Rome. Somewhere in the middle of the appalling turmoil Marco's family lost everything. His parents died, and he was left to fend for himself as best he could. He can't have been more than twelve or thirteen years old. Think of all the films that came out after the war—*Shoeshine* and *Bicycle Thief* and *Miracle in Milan*. Marco must have known poverty like that. Rome in the fifties is such a lovely place now, it's hard for us to realize what it must have been like then.

Somehow Marco managed to survive, but of course he couldn't forget. He wanted desperately to feel safe again. Always at the back of his mind there must have been that three o'clock in the morning fear of plunging down to the depths again. I ought to have realized earlier how important security and power were to Marco. Perhaps I did realize it, and wouldn't admit it."

"His family would have b-brought him up to expect a p-position of p-power in the world?" said Stephen.

"Yes, but they couldn't give him the means of achieving it. He'd have had a gentleman's education, so I suppose that even as a boy of twelve he spoke French and English, was a good shot, and had nice manners. Then came the crash, and all that came to an end."

"How did he get into films?" asked Hal.

"I don't know," said Emma. "But he soon found that it had certain advantages. He told me once that he discovered very early on that he didn't need to spend much money on food, because there'd always be a sympathetic waitress in the studio canteen who'd let him eat and drink for free. And he didn't need to spend a lot of money on smart clothes, because nobody wears smart clothes on the set—and if he needed to look elegant for some special occasion, there'd always be a sympathetic girl in Wardrobe who'd lend him clothes from stock."

"And when he needed to know the English technical terms used in film-making," said Hal, "there was a sympathetic Continuity Girl wanting to improve her Italian and happy to teach him technical English in exchange."

"Yes," said Emma. "When the Americans began making films in Italy, Marco found himself being promoted over the heads of older and more experienced men, simply because he spoke English and they didn't. Before long he was on quite close terms with big American directors and film stars. And to Marco they represented power."

"The real power," said Hal, "lies not in Rome but in the States."

"Exactly," said Emma. "And that's where he wanted to be."

"Aren't the Americans always here?" said Stephen.

"No," said Emma. "I think it started when America passed some law a few years ago splitting up production and distribution of films. I don't quite understand it, but at the moment American film-makers come here in droves because it's cheaper to set up productions here than it is in the States, and besides they get tax concessions and things. But all that could disappear any time. This year, next year, the Americans could pull out, and Marco knew it. When that happened, he'd be at the bottom of the pile, one of a hundred out-of-works scrambling for every job. So he was desperate to latch on to somebody who could get him in with the top people in Hollywood. He tried Stella, but she turned him down—she understood what he was really after."

"I thought that Stella was making a play for Marco," said Hal. "I see now that it was the other way about. She turned him down, and took up with that gondolier."

"And soon after that," said Emma, "Leonidas arrived with Ariadne."

A hush fell on them as they recalled the moment they had first seen Ariadne standing at the top of the Venetian staircase, a shy, exquisite child with long red-gold hair. Emma remembered the big close-up in the gondola, when Ariadne opened her eyes and sent shivers of ecstasy through anyone in her line of vision.

"And Walther said that Ariadne would have had Stella's part if she'd arrived earlier," said Hal.

"Yes," said Emma. "That must have been Stella's death-warrant. Marco was already friendly with Leonidas and Ariadne. They relied on him for advice, because he knew the film business and they didn't. If Ariadne replaced Stella, then Marco would be the power behind the rising star."

"So he killed Stella," said Hal. "It was easy. All he had to do was to pick up a lunch-box. Any lunch-box. Put some poison on the pastry—he probably did that in Karl's office, where nobody could see him. Then he gave the box to Stella."

"She had no more shooting to do that afternoon," said Emma. "If she'd been taken ill on the set, the company doctor would have been called and her life just might have been saved. But she was taken ill on a deserted island with only the gondolier to look after her—and *he* thought at first that she was just drunk."

"Marco must have had a bad time waiting for the gondola to return, you know what I mean," said Dave the stunt man.

"And I was so indignant when the police took Marco away," said Emma.

"So was I," said Hal.

"Smatterafact, we all were," said Johnny. "Everyone liked Marco, and none of us cared much about Stella."

"But we did care about Leonidas, you know what I mean," said Dave.

They fell silent again, remembering. Leonidas rehearsing his stunts with Dave and Johnny. Leonidas getting wrapped up in the wire belonging to the trick bolt. Leonidas laughing. And then, suddenly, unbelievably, Leonidas dead.

"At first," said Emma, "I suspected Richard and Yorky of killing Leonidas."

"What possible reason could they have had?" exploded Dave.

"Richard was afraid that Leonidas would outshine him," said Emma. "I thought Yorky missed the hand-hold deliberately."

"To give Richard a chance to switch the bolts?" said Hal.

"That's right," said Emma.

"Emma—is that why you went up on the battlements?" he asked.

"How did you know about that?" asked Emma, surprised.

"Richard told me," said Hal, and he grinned. "Said he and

Yorky were worried—said you obviously had no head for heights—and said he had some crazy conversation with you about Pinocchio."

Emma flushed.

"I was wrong," she said, and heard once again the whisper of the great bell of the Torre Mangia: WRONG . . . WRONG . . . WRONG . . .

"Yorky missed the hand-hold," said Dave bluntly, "because he's getting old. But of course he couldn't admit it—Karl would have kicked him off the picture, you know what I mean . . ."

There was a murmur of agreement from the stunt men.

"So Yorky pretended the hand-hold was broken, or something," said Hal. "Said it must be replaced."

"And Marco," said Emma, "found himself with the means of killing Leonidas to his hand."

"Yes," said Hal. "He waited until the new hand-hold was fixed. Everybody left the set. He doubled back. Switched the bolts. Set off the smoke-pot in the stables. Strolled into the barn for lunch and waited for the stable-lad to raise the alarm of a fire."

"I told him I suspected Richard and Yorky," said Emma. "How he must have laughed . . ."

"I suppose Marco could see that Ariadne was heading for the big time," said Dave. "He planned to kill Leonidas and marry her himself?"

"Yes," said Emma, "but I believe that Ariadne put the idea into his head. And what's more I believe she gave him the idea of getting rid of Stella Camay."

There was a babble of disbelief from the men.

Emma said, "With Stella out of the way, Ariadne had the chance of becoming a star, and with Leonidas out of the way she had a chance of becoming Mrs. Walther Meister. She must have been well aware from the start that Walther had fallen in love with her. She was just as ambitious as Marco. Marriage into the Meister family would take her right to the top. All she had to do was to look like the innocent flower and behave like the serpent under it, a course of conduct recommended by Lady Macbeth."

"Sheer guesswork," said Hal. "Not a shred of evidence."

"What's h-happened to Ariadne?" asked Stephen.

"She's gone to the States," said Penny the Production Secretary. "She's still under contract. Karl said he needed her for dubbing and publicity. She went on the same plane as Richard and his wife. I don't think Richard's wife was terribly pleased about it . . . ."

She lit a fresh cigarette from the stub of her previous one. Emma looked at the stub as Penny ground it out in the ashtray.

"Setting fire to the tower at La Rocca," she said in a small voice. "I suppose that was Marco?"

"Afraid so, Emma," said Hal.

"B-but why should he d-do it?" said Stephen. "Why should he want to k-kill Emma? Emma was his friend."

"I don't know whether this has anything to do with it," said Emma slowly. "The day before we returned to La Rocca, Walther announced that he was going to marry Ariadne. Well, a little later I overheard Marco having a terrible row with Ariadne. At first it was just a blur of shouting, two Italians having a disagreement, but at the end I heard him say, "Do you want me to tell Mr. Meister about Klara Sauss?" Then he came out of Ariadne's trailer and saw me."

"Klara Sauss!" exclaimed Penny.

"That's right," said Emma. "Sauss as in Strauss. Does the name mean anything to you?"

Penny nodded.

"Yes," she said. "But I hadn't realized that Marco knew about it."

"Who is Klara Sauss?" asked Emma.

"Klara Sauss is the way the Italians pronounce it," said Penny. "The English call it Clara's House. It's the name of a

Venetian brothel. Ariadne worked there before she married Leonidas."

"You mean—Ariadne had been a prostitute?" said Emma. The men were loudly incredulous, but Penny was adamant.

"So Stella was right after all!" cried Stephen. "D-don't you remember that awful d-day when she looked at Ariadne sitting b-beside Walther and said—and said . . ."

He blushed uncomfortably at the memory.

"She said something about Ariadne being a child-whore," said Emma. "I thought it was just Stella being outrageous."

"Perhaps she was," said Penny, "but she was close to the truth. I knew Ariadne had worked at Clara's House, because I saw it on her documents in the office. And her real name wasn't Ariadne, and until she married Leonidas she wasn't Greek, she was Italian."

"But why didn't you tell somebody?" said Emma.

"It was none of my business," said Penny. "Good heavens, if I started talking about the things I've read on people's documents I'd never get any work done. Quite apart from the fact that such things are supposed to be confidential. You know as well as I do that nobody in the film business ever has a past—and if they have, they'll thank you not to mention it."

"So what you overheard, Emma, was Marco threatening to tell Walther about Ariadne's past," said Hal. "That might not have worried him—but *he couldn't know how much else you might have heard.* He'd probably said enough to give you a very clear picture of his guilt. So you were dangerous. So he set fire to the tower."

"But in that case," said Emma, "why didn't he try to kill me at the Palio? I was in his sights. In fact, I thought the gun was aimed at me. But he only fired one shot, the one that killed Walther. Then he pulled the gun back through the grille. I was a perfect target. Why didn't he shoot me too?"

"I think I c-can answer that," said Stephen. He spoke slowly, as though feeling his way. "You see, after Emma jumped from the b-burning tower, I met M-Marco, and he was c-crying. He was b-badly shocked. Well, I m-mean, we all were, b-but once we knew that you were safe, Emma, we all felt b-better. But M-Marco *stayed* shocked."

"He'd already killed two people," said Hal. "Why was this different?"

"I think," said Stephen hesitantly, "this was the first time he'd seen one of his v-victims suffering. Stella m-must have endured agonies on the island, but by the time M-Marco had to look at her, it was all over, and she was dead. And Leonidas was k-killed before M-Marco returned to the set. They were both d-deaths at a d-distance—as unreal as d-deaths on a cinema screen. But Emma in d-danger of b-burning to d-death —that he had to watch. And I think he suddenly saw what he had b-become."

"And he couldn't live with that knowledge?" said Hal.

"I think he m-made up his mind to prevent Walther m-marrying Ariadne, but once he'd done that, he d-didn't care what happened."

"After Marco fired at Walther," said Hal, "a couple of carabinieri went after him. He dropped the gun, ran up the stairs to the bell-tower. He knew there was only one way out for him, and he took it."

A distant clock chimed. Hal put his glass down on the table.

"I expect you are right, Emma, about Marco being driven by fear to do what he did. But I think there was another reason as well. It was pride. I should have known," said Hal. "I should have *known* there was something wrong. When Marco talked to me about his interview at the Questura, I asked him if he'd been hurt—you see, I thought they might have duffed him up a bit. But he said only his pride had been hurt. And not because he was suspected of murder, but *because he had to admit to a policeman that he carried lunch-boxes*—'like a servant,' he said. That's when I should have known that something was wrong. Most people would be far more upset at being suspected of murder than of behaving like a servant. I think Marco's very old family brought him up to believe that other people's lives didn't really matter. The honour of the family—that was the most important thing."

He took a deep breath.

"Who am I to talk?" said Hal. "When Stephen suggested we ought to do something about Stella's death, I refused to listen. I thought that getting the film made was the most important thing. Making the film—that was my first priority. Even when Leonidas died—even when Emma nearly died, I wanted to believe that it was an accident . . ."

His glance travelled round them all, and came to rest on Stephen.

"You were right, Stephen," he said. "You said that human life must come first. You were right . . ."

He sat staring at the ground, ashamed to meet their eyes. Emma laid her hand upon his shoulder, and he reached up and gripped it. There was silence, and then a little breeze stirred the jasmine, and a single star-shaped blossom fluttered down from the trellis and settled like a snowflake on the hand of Dave the stunt man.

"Time we were going," he said.

He stood up, looking first at the jasmine flower in his hand and then at the buildings beyond the trellis—the Colosseum and the Forum, the dome of St. Peter's, the "wedding-cake" memorial—each of them a monument to power in its own age. Rome, the Eternal City.

"It's the same on every picture," said Dave. "Four months ago we arrived in Venice, over a hundred of us, all strangers to each other. You made us into a team, Hal. A good team. And you held us together when we might have fallen apart—you know what I mean . . ."

There was a murmur of agreement, and Hal slowly raised his head, but he kept his hold on Emma's hand.

"And now we're all scattering," said Dave. "We'll probably never see each other again. František and the camera crew—"

"Richard and Yorky," said Johnny.

"Hairdressing, Wardrobe and Make-Up," said Penny.

"B-Brock B-Berowne," said Stephen.

"All scattered," said Dave. "Seems a waste, somehow . . ."

He flicked the small white flower over the trellis and watched it spiral down and away over the rooftops.

"We'd better go," he said, "or I shall find myself making a speech. But you know what I mean. Ciao, Emma!"

There was a flurry of farewells, and Stephen found himself crammed into the antiquated little lift which slowly groaned its way to earth.

Dave and Johnny led the way towards the Piazza del Popolo. Traffic roared past them. Vespa scooters buzzed and swooped. Pedestrians darted through the cars, exchanging insults with drivers and greetings with friends. After the calm of Lucca, walking across the Piazza del Popolo was like going over Niagara in a barrel.

"Where shall we eat?" asked Dave, pausing for a moment. "Ottavio's?"

"Fine," said Penny, and the stunt men agreed.

"What about you, Steve?" said Dave.

Stephen glowed. It was the first time anybody had ever called him Steve. He felt that he was one of the team. He turned to tell Hal, and then for the first time he noticed that Hal was not with them. He must have stayed behind with Emma. Stephen was about to remark on this when he thought better of it. A man of the world called Steve knew when to keep his mouth shut . . .

Early the following year the film appeared on cinema screens throughout the world. Like a hard-riding jockey in the Palio, Karl Meister had flogged *The Trumpets of Tuscany* through months of editing, post-production and sneak previews, and brought it storming to the finishing post. The verdict of the judges was unanimous. It was a winner.

"It's a Meisterpiece!" trumpeted one critic.

"A Star Is Born—and her name is Ariadne Andros!" said another.

Their only complaint was directed at the unconvincing death-fall from the top of the bell-tower—"obviously a stuffed dummy," they said.

But they all loved Ariadne. They wrote panegyrics about the long Minnehaha procession, and the slowly falling blossoms on the black ship, and they hugged to themselves the moment of ecstasy, when Ariadne opened her eyes in the big close-up and looked straight at them.

The public loved Ariadne too. They loved the whole film.

Richard attended the Hollywood première with his wife.

Brock attended the London première with a good friend.

Emma, Hal and the rest of the crew didn't get around to seeing the picture at all. Nobody invited them to a première, and anyhow by that time they were all working on other films, and *The Trumpets of Tuscany* was only a memory.

Stephen didn't see it either. He was working hard on his book. He hadn't sold it to anyone yet, but a publisher had said that he might be interested in it if the film won an Oscar, and Stephen was an incurable optimist.

The next year Emma chanced to pick up a magazine with a cover picture of the Oscar awards. Inside was a photograph of L. J. Hacker clutching a gold statuette.

Emma blinked. It couldn't be true . . .

The Trumpets of Tuscany had won the award for the Best Screenplay. A hotch-potch cobbled together from six different scripts, half the scenes not even properly worked out but scribbled on old envelopes, scraps of paper, and a sheet of toilet paper. The Best Screenplay!

Another photograph showed Karl and Ariadne clasping similar statuettes. The caption read: "Karl Meister won the Best Director award for *The Trumpets of Tuscany*. The award for the Best Female Newcomer went to Ariadne Andros (in private life Mrs. Karl Meister) for her role in the same film."

Mrs. Karl Meister. . . So Ariadne had made it to the top after all!

Never under-estimate the power of a woman, thought Emma wryly.

Then she went cold all over as she remembered comparing Ariadne to Lady Macbeth. "Sheer guesswork," Hal had said. "Not a shred of evidence."

But surely Karl Meister already had a wife?

Yes, her name was Minna, and she had been crazy about the Palio.

So—what had happened to Minna?

Emma closed her eyes, and a voice, faint and faraway, whispered in her ear:

"The thane of Fife had a wife; where is she now?"

ABOUT THE AUTHOR

Hazel Wynn Jones has spent most of her professional life in the film business. She began as a Script Supervisor (then known as a Continuity Girl in England) on international features made in England, France, Germany, and—most of all—Italy. She worked with such famous stars as Brigitte Bardot, Robert Taylor, Gregory Peck, and Audrey Hepburn. Later she became a scriptwriter and director of shorts and documentary films. It is perhaps not surprising that the heroine of *Death and the Trumpets of Tuscany,* her Crime Club debut, is a Continuity Girl who hopes one day to become a film director.